Henry Cholmondeley-Pennell

'From grave to gay'

A volume of selections from the complete poems

Henry Cholmondeley-Pennell

'From grave to gay'
A volume of selections from the complete poems

ISBN/EAN: 9783337206246

Printed in Europe, USA, Canada, Australia, Japan

Cover: Foto ©Andreas Hilbeck / pixelio.de

More available books at **www.hansebooks.com**

'FROM GRAVE TO GAY'

A VOLUME OF SELECTIONS FROM

THE COMPLETE POEMS

H. CHOLMONDELEY-PENNELL

Author of 'Puck on Pegasus' 'Pegasus Re-saddled'
'Modern Babylon' &c.

LONDON

LONGMANS, GREEN, AND CO

NEW YORK

GEORGE J. COOMBES

5 EAST SEVENTEENTH STREET

1884

TO

ALFRED, LORD TENNYSON,

POET LAUREATE,

THESE PAGES ARE PRIVILEGED TO BE
DEDICATED AS A MEMENTO OF MANY
PLEASANT HOURS OF PERSONAL INTER-
COURSE, AND IN LOVE AND ADMIRATION
OF HIS GENIUS.

H. CHOLMONDELEY-PENNELL.

20 *May* 1884.

Erratum.

Page 58, line 2, *for* Thomas *read* George.

PART I.

MY VIS-À-VIS.

YOUR step is the softest that brushes
    The silken-swept floors of Cockayne,
Your face is the idol they worship
    In Fashion's idolatrous fane :
Did fancy recall for the moment
    We pass'd in the dazzling throng,
A wave-lighted darkness by Arno,
    And one lonely fisherman's song ?
Some sweetnesses whispered at parting,
    Some clasping of hands when we met ?—
Or have you forgot to remember
    What I—recollect to forget ?

A folly !—but good while it lasted,—
    Perhaps we've grown wiser since then ;
You're learned in the highways and byways
    Of the paths of the children of men.
The blossoms and fruits of Love's garden
    The star-flow'rs that vanish with morn —
Are not for my Eve of the Arno . . .
    I've found that the ' rose has a thorn.'

Then was Paradise undisenchanted,
   Young Love a divinity yet,—
Now, you can forget to remember
   Whilst I—recollect to forget.

There are scores only asking permission
   To put their necks under your foot,
The slaves of your sceptre, my beauty,
   Outnumber the slaves of Amroot.
Yet still as you stand in the glitter,
   The pride and the passion of pow'r,
Sigh once for the glory departed,
   The love that you loved—for an hour :
The stars we saw rise upon Arno
   Shall turn in their courses and set,
Before you forget to remember
   Or I . . . recollect to forget !

THE SECRET OF SAFETY.

YOU ask me to declare the spell
     By which I sleep unhaunted slumbers:
' Still fancy free !—the secret tell ? '
The secret is, fair Floribel,
     That Safety lies in numbers.

It is not that my heart is tough,
     I dare not make such false confession,
Or that it's formed of such soft stuff
It is not durable enough
     To keep a firm impression :

But Beauty's like the bloom that flies,
     And Love's a butterfly that hasteth ;
From lip to lip the trifler hies
And sweet by sweet the garden tries,
     But each one only tasteth. . . .

If long I loiter'd here, I know
     I might not sleep unhaunted slumbers,
At least 'twere rash to try, fair Flo'—
So now I'm going to the Row,
     Where ' Safety lies in numbers ! '

LITTLE BO-PEEP.

' LITTLE Bo-peep has lost her sheep,'
   And some one or other's lost little Bo-peep—
Or she'd never be wand'ring at twelve o'clock
With a golden crook, and a velvet frock,
In a diamond necklace, in such a rout,—
In diamond buckles, and high-heel'd shoes
(And a dainty wee foot in them too, if you choose,
And an ankle a sculptor might rave about. . . .)
But I think she's a little witch, you know,
With her broomstick-crook and her high-heel'd shoe
And the mischievous fun that flashes thro'
The wreaths of her amber hair—don't you?
No wonder the flock follows little Bo-peep,—
Such a shepherd would turn all the world into sheep,
To trot at her heels and look up in the face
Of their pastor for—goodness knows what, say for
    grace?—
Her face that recalls in its reds and its blues,
And its setting of gold, ' Esmeralda ' by Greuze. . . .

There you've Little Bo-peep, dress, diamonds, and all,
As I met her last night at the Fancy Ball.

'FAITE À PEINDRE.'

'MADE to be painted'—a Millais might give
    A fortune to study that exquisite face—
The face is a fortune—a Lawrence might live
    Anew in each line of that figure's still grace.

The pose is perfection, a model each limb,
    From the delicate foot to the classical head ;
But the almond blue eyes, with their smiling, look dim,
    And lips to be *loved* want a trifle more red.

Statuesque? no, a Psyche, let's say, in repose,
    A Psyche whose Cupid beseeches in vain,
We sigh as the nightingale sighs to the rose
    That declines (it's averred) to give sighs back
        again. . . .

If the wind shook the rose? then a shower would fall
    Of sweet-scented petals to gather who list ;
If a sigh shook my Psyche? she'd yawn, that is all,
    She's made to be painted—and not to be kist.

A CASE OF SPOONS.

(He)

I WONDER why to sit I find it sweet,
As if you were Gamaliel, at your feet?
They're quite too small to be of any use?—

(She)

Because you are a goose.

(He) I wonder, when your glances downward stray,
Why mine look up until yours turn away—
You hate the sight of me, I dare assert!

(She)

Because I hate a flirt.

(He) Then tell me why, when you attempt to speak,
I find my ear gets closer to your cheek,
Until it almost touches some one's locks?

(She)

Because it wants a box!

TO AN ANONYMOUS CORRESPONDENT.

NO name—unknown the ' hand '—and yet
   I think your fingers must be taper
Who wrote ' *non ti scordar*,' and set
   This tiny seal on pink-ting'd paper?

The page is fair, and deftly traced ;
   Folded across and neatly dated :
The p's and q's display much taste ;
   The h's look well aspirated.

The i's are—well, like sweet sixteen's--
   When laughter's light and smiles are plenty .   .
My taste's Moresque, or so, for queens—
   I'm sure you can't be more than twenty?

You still are in the bloom of youth
   With faultless face and figure fairy,
They call you ' Blanche ' or ' Maud '—in sooth
   The odds are ten to one on ' Mary !'

If e'er we meet in after-life
   Speak, dear—I'll answer circumspectly :
And tho' you're some one else's wife,
   You still might spell my name correctly?

PRETTY PUSS.

THE slightest of pouts on the softest of lips
    Of a little red mouth with its smiles in eclipse
The least little flash under eyelids half shut,
The least little beat of the least little foot,
Like the thrill of the tigress preparing to spring,—
Seem to hint that my Mabel is not quite the thing? . .

I wish I were back in the hansom for choice !—
Shall I fight? or, like Niobe, lift up my voice ?
Own my conduct was vile (but I've done that before),
Cry *Peccavi!* and never offend any more?
Or brazen it out ?—' Yes, I trifled with Jane,
And I flirted with Flo, and—I mean to again !'—

Tableau!—But I'll keep on this side of the table,
There's certainly something that's cat-like in Mabel,—
If stroked the right way you get plenty of purr,
But claws, on occasion, lie hid in the fur,
And ready to come ' to the scratch,' you may swear,
As the Irishman's coat-tails at Donnybrook Fair. . . .

It's perplexing—I wish I were back in the cab. . . .
There's something remarkably *cat-like* in Mab.

LEASES FOR WIVES;

OR, WHAT WE'RE COMING TO

A PARTNERSHIP for life—absurd !
　　How droll—a wedding ring !
Somehow *we* don't perceive the fun ;
' For seven, fourteen, or twenty-one,'
　　Is now the style of thing.

We meet our charmer in the Row ;
　　One glance !—'tis love at sight—
We meet again at rout or hop,
A valse, two ices, and then pop,—
　　Boulogne to-morrow night.

No trousseau cumbers up the fair
　　With heaps of costly trash ;
No wedding breakfast makes her ill,
Nor speeches, that won't pay the bill,
　　Nor ' settlements' of cash.

We register no fees on earth,
　　No vows record in heaven :
A sheet of cream-laid note—'tis done !
For seven, fourteen, or twenty-one . . .
　　Suppose we try for *seven ?*

FORTY-FIVE.

HOW is it that I'm forty-five
    And still so very much unmarried?
Why did I wait so long to wive,
    Or was it that the Ladies tarried?

I rather think that as a boy
    My notions were not celibatic;
At fourteen I was scarcely coy
    But dreamt of heav'n in an attic,—

With Katy, *ætat.* thirty-two,
    And wrote her an amazing ditty;
' My heart for her should still be true '-
    And she refused it—heartless Kitty!

I did not weep! if she'd said ' yes '
    It might have been a theme for laughter:
My sufferings led me to confess
    To Mary Anne a fortnight after.

Poor Poll! (I call you so because
    No sense of injury now rankles—)
I think our *casus spooni* was
    You had such pretty feet and ankles?

Præterea nil! might end the clause,
    Tho' that would be ungallant, very . . .
Lizette had elephantine paws
    But cheeks as rosy as a cherry.

Louisa next—my little Loo !—
    Whose hand I claimed with fervent kisses
Unluckily these things take *two*,
    And *one* declined becoming ' Missis.'

A time arrives when every man
    Has fatuous feelings for a cousin,
And if the first ' draws blank ' he can
    (At least I did) try half a dozen ;—

First, second, third—still no success—
    Fourth, fifth, and sixth, the numbers ran on ·
Not one my lonely lot would bless,
    And two were contrary to the canon.

At last, *at last !* my pulse still stirs
    As I recall thy vision, Dora !
The rose-bud lip that owned me hers—
    The brow suggestive of Aurora ;

I swore that we should never part,
    Nor time nor change our love make colder,
I clasped her to my beating heart . . .
    And ran my scarf-pin in her shoulder !

The temper's warm at 'sweet sixteen';
  We parted more in wrath than sorrow;
And Dora's married Jack since then,
  It's just ten years ago to-morrow.

And now life's chords no music wake,
  I'm getting in the sere and yellow,
Is there no womankind will take
  Compassion on a lonely fellow?

Some Dora with less scornful eyes?
  I think I've still some love to give her—
No more scarf-pins I'll patronise
  But stick to Rings, henceforth for ever.

A LITTLE BEAUTY.

MAUD's a naughty little girl,
 Maudie's locks decline to curl,
  Spite all sense of duty,
But they're *fris'd* up instead
Round her saucy little head,
Round her cheeks of white and red
  Maud's a little beauty !

Maud has got a roguish eye,
Maud has got a tender sigh,
  Laughters soft and flutey—
' Cherries ripe ' her lips, I swear,
Did you ever know a pair
Say so plainly ' If you dare ! '—
  Maud the little beauty !

Yet her lip you cannot reach
Nor her cheek that's like a peach,
  Round and ripe and fruity.
You can only look and sigh,—
I can only love, and try
To discern the reason why
  Maud's *my* little beauty ?

A GORDIAN KNOT.

A HANDKERCHIEF—dropt out, you say,
    From the receptacle allotted ? . . .
Not much if that were all, but stay,
    This pocket-handkerchief is *knotted*—

There at one end—frail souvenir,
    Hinting the need of mental tonics ;
Whence comes the pale preceptor here
    To give his lesson in mnemonics ?

Is it from him whose ' un-urned ' shade
    Petitions that, instead of joking,
The debt of kinship should be paid
    To-day at Kensal Green or Woking ?

Poor Tom ! you were not much to me,
    A cousin, twice removed, by marriage,
Removed once more by fate's decree—
    At any rate I'll send the carriage. . . .

Or, query, was it ' him ' at all ?
    This true-love knot may be a token
Of some fair vision I'd recall—
    Of faithless vows and promise broken ?

Love's tryst unkept by haunted well ;
 Its sweet forget-me-nots forgotten. . . .
Perhaps it's only some one's bill
 I back'd ?—of course it turned out rotten, –

Or hint to pay that bet I owe
 For views about the Derby winner ;
I'd rather much it was to go
 To Greenwich for a whitebait dinner ! . . .

Of pay or play may preach this knot—
 Of death or duns or love's emotion—
I tied it yesterday, but what
 It means, I've not the faintest notion !

FIVE YEARS' CHARACTER.

FIVE years, *amie!* five years ago,
　　It seems like yesterday,
You whispered that mysterious vow—
　　Love—honour—and obey.
And, darling, you have done your part,
　　And kept your promise, sweet,—
You have full-filled an empty heart
　　And made a life complete . . .
I testify that you have been
The household sunshine, fairy, queen,-
A cool oasis ever green
　　Along life's deserts sandy,—
　　　　As good as gold,
　　　　As true as steel,
　　And as sweet as sugar candy !

We've shared some pleasure and some pain,
　　We've met some ups and downs :
And would you tie the knot again
　　Tho' all the smiles were frowns ? . . .
Tho' all the joys were griefs, I say,
　　And dimmed each brighter spot,
This girl would face them all with me,—
　　You would, love, would you not ?

And still would be what you have been,
My household fairy, sunshine, queen--
A cool oasis ever green
   Amidst life's deserts sandy, —
      As good as gold,
      As true as steel,
   And as sweet as sugar candy.

LADY 'BELL'S CATECHISM.

WHAT are your 'load-stars,' sir?
      ' My Bella's eyes : '
And what's the sweetest of ' sweet air ' ?
      ' Her sighs : '
Where does the ' bee suck ' ?
      ' From her honey'd lip,
(Wish I'd the luck,
      Just a rewarding sip !')
Who ' smiles and smiles,' and not one false ?
      ' My sweet : '
What look as if they ' dreamed a valse ' ?
      ' Her feet : '
What is her arm ?
      ' A Wreath as moonlight fair : '
Her hand, ' so white, so warm ' ?
      ' A sceptre rare —
(The only one to which I bow,
      My pet !')
Stuff ! pay attention now,
      And don't forget : —

Where is the 'glass of fashion'?
  'In her eye!' . . .
(You'll put me in a passion
  If you try!—)
What is the 'mould of form,' then?
  'Bella's bonnet:'
Good gracious! Tom,
  I think you're sitting on it!) . . .
What is each 'wayward fancy's sport'?
  'The moon:'
Nonsense, it's nothing of the sort
  'A spoon:'
What's 'changeless yet tho' all should change
  ('Hullo!
I say, this grass is getting damp, you know!')
A 'thing of beauty and a joy,' what is it, tell?
 'My loved and loving, lovely lady 'Bell!'

THE SQUIRE AND THE NEW PARSON'S GIRL.

WITH wild locks streaming from the braid
   That fillets them in vain,
Who is this hatless demoisel
   Comes flying down the lane—
It must be our new parson's girl,
   I think they call her Jane? . . .

They really shouldn't let her out
   In such prepost'rous guise—
Sixteen ! and in a pinafore
   Suggestive of 'dirt pies' !
Frock'd to the knee ! . . . and what a pair
   Of great blue saucer eyes !

The fair Miss Jenny's future lord
   Will need to have a care !—
Despite the piquant little nose
   'Tip-tilted' in the air—
They glitter like two corn-flow'rs thro'
   That hayfield of her hair.

And then her mouth ! a mile too wide
  But arched like Cupid's bow,
And strung with pearls—I never saw
  Such a surprising row :
All womankind might ' show their teeth '
  If they'd such teeth to show.

'Twould almost be worth while to make
  The little vixen scold,
If but to see the scornful smile
  Flash out so bright and bold. . . .
There isn't such a face for miles,
  Though half the shire were poll'd.

And face and figure ought to match,
  Or nature's made a slip ;
She looks as flexible and straight
  As my new riding-whip—
Upon my word if she'd a chance
  I think she'd like to skip. . . .

And I should like to hold the rope
  Tho' skipping's not my way :
She leads them all a pretty life
  Up at the Grange, they say . . .
It's really rude not to have called .
  I think I'll go to-day.

SOME ONE'S FORGET-ME-NOTS.

SOME one's Forget-me-nots !
 ' Laid up in lavender '—
Gew-gaws and trash and stuff—
Billets-doux—rhymes enough—
 Love's ritornellas ;—
Here's an odd shoe of pink
Once in fate's chain a link,
So small one fain would think
 'Twas Cinderella's.

Two lace-trimmed handkerchiefs,
Six rosettes !—fie for shame !
Clearly the youthful flame
 Went in for slippers ;
Three gloves—some locks of hair. . . .
I wonder whose they were ?
But at least one may swear
 They were all ' clippers.'

What's this perfume that comes
Faint as I close the lid ?
Have I locked up instead
 Somebody's posy ?

Stay, I believe that it's
These crumpled violets,
Heartsease and mignonettes,
    Rosebuds once rosy :

Ready-made *pot-pourri*—
(Sweet-scented none the less)
Isn't it time all this
    Rubbish were rotten ?
Ribbons and gloves and locks . . .
Never mind, shut the box—
    Lie still in lavender,
Some one's Forget-me-nots,
    Long since forgotten !

A CURL IN A LETTER.

A LETTER, and a yellow curl,—
    That's plain—the rest is left for guesses :
Who's this romantic little girl
    That plays Delilah with her tresses?

For *me* ! who never cared a rap
    For rounded waist or taper ankle,--
At whom no spinster sets her cap,
    No Cupid shoots the shafts that rankle !

' My dear—I grieve to make you pout—
    But still it is imprudent, very,
To show'r your golden gifts about
    In this way on Dick, Tom, and Harry ;

' No doubt you've charms you highly prize
    Or else you'd scarce be Adam's daughter, ·
There may be death in your blue eyes,
    But—don't affect promiscuous slaughter.' . .

Well preach'd ! but somehow scarcely *nice* ? --
    And letters lead to tittle-tattle ;
I think one ought to give advice
    Vive voix—the tone is half the battle ?

'Twould not be hard to *match* this curl
  But should I like its fellow better? . . .
. . . You very yellow-pated girl
  Who wrote me this romantic letter.

AT BRINDISI.

ON BOARD THE " P AND O."

I CAN'T say much for ' Brindisi the blest,'
   As one poor lady called it who was sick,
But yet to English eyes it boasts a charm,
A strip of deep green grass—that after sand
And olive-tinted fields and groves and trees,
Comes with a cool refreshing hope of home.

   And tranquilly beside the ' Pera ' lies,
As glad to rest after her long sea-strife ;
But all upon her deck is bustling stir,
For last *A Dios* wished, hand-shakings past,
And civil stewardess ' tipped ' like Dian's shafts,
Each one just now is looking after one,—
Excepting Benedick, who seeks his spouse
Not yet emerged from cabin mysteries,
And charges up the trunk-encumber'd poop,
Regardless of his own or others' neck
Or long-backed chairs that bump his faithful legs.

   There goes our gay grass-widow whom they call
The ' Stormy Petrel,' for she tells her friends
There's always some disaster when she sails ;

And she has sailed three times with Captain Jack,
And every time a damage or a loss—
A twisted axle or a broken screw —
And when he saw her on the gangway last
At Alexandria, crying ' Now I've come
Captain, look out for squalls ! ' he was so mad
They thought he'd send her back ; but all went well
For some one hid a horseshoe in her berth. . . .

And there's the stout Mynheer who always wears
A patent air-belt underneath his coat
And loaded pistols, ready primed to shoot
The thief, who in the wreck and strain for life,
Would filch his prize   his belt. . . .
                            And once they made
Pretence that we must sink, and this fat man,
Too scant of breath t' inflate the saviour bag,
Went rushing madly up and down the ship
Beseeching every one ' Give me von blow ! '

Our pets are going too—the pale-faced ape
Who look'd so mild but bit me to the bone ;
The Colonel's pug, and Mop, and last not least,
The cockatoo who called poor Bishop Smith
' A (naughty word) old fool,' and had to be
Removed for laughing, when his Lordship read
The Sunday Service on the quarter-deck. . . .

Going, going, gone ! and I'm the last that's left,
Perched like a Jew amongst a heap of coats :
Well, good-bye all ! and good-bye too, my May,
For here comes Gus to say the train is in.

DAISY'S DIGIT.

O FINGER with the circlet slight,
  That keeps it warm and cosy,
Wee winsome third left-handed doight
  So white and warm and rosy, —
More taper digits there may be,
  More lips may kiss and cling on,
This tiny finger's best to me—
  The one I put the ring on.

Some fingers may perhaps proclaim
  A precedence of *status*,
To point the shaft of praise or blame
  Or scorn at those that hate us ;
Lay down the law, you counsel small !
  Your barbèd arrows string on !
To me this finger's best of all—
  The one I put the ring on.

My finger has not worked a bit
  In caligraphies dainty,
The busy thimble dares not fit
  The type of Suzerainty, —

Such weapons of bewild'ring art
I have no wit to sing on,
This fairy finger holds my heart —
The one I put the ring on.

LONDON'S 'SUEZ CANAL.'

WHAT pretty girls one sees about !
　　At rink and race, at ball and rout,
　　　　At drums and dinners,
In books, where Ænids find Geraints,
In pictures Mr. Millais paints,
In church I'm fond of such young saints
　　　　Or sinners.

A score at least one's sure to meet
From Charing Cross to Oxford Street,
　　　　Or climbing hilly
St. James's, where of clubdom sick,
Old fogeys voted at old Nick
Fond glances turn at 4 towards Pic-
　　　　·cadilly.

Muse-favoured haunt of all that's gay !
Whose every stone has had its day
　　　　Of loves and graces !
Your triumphs many a bard can tell,
Fred Locker sings them passing well,
I know you bear away the bell
　　　　For faces.

D

Along your strand converging flow
The social tides to Rotten Row,
      Beloved and shady ;
Old Gouty trundles with his ' pair,'
De Boodle saunters, cane in air,
And wonders who's that golden hair-
        'd young lady ? . . .

But whether gold or black or grey
Fashion decrees her slaves shall say
      The *dernier goût* is,
You bear your motley freightage well,
And East and West your convoys swell, —
A sort of cockneyfied canal
      Of Suez !

A neutral ' cut,' where every man's
A vessel bound to pay the trans-
      -it dues and duty,—
Dues stricter than e'er Lesseps took,—
Love's tribute levied on a look —
And duly noted in the book
      Of Beauty.

And now, whilst ice enwraps you still,
And snow's on Constitution Hill
      Like some old Pharaoh,

Sun-shaded mid the fervent rays,
I bask away the balmy days
And write these verses to your praise
      In Cairo.

All here's aglow with summer sun
There hugs black frost his mantle dun
      In winter chilly :
Yet could I stand on ' Simla's ' deck
And westward . . . ere this watch's tick
Old England ho ! for me, and Pic-
      -cadilly !

'A POCKET VENUS.'

MABEL isn't quite fifteen,
　　She's just like some dolls I've seen —
　　　　Could they mischief mean us ;
Two red lips my doll has got,
Eyes like blue forget-me-not,
Flaxen ringlets—such a lot ! —
　　　　May's my pocket Venus.

May has got a figure fine
Tho' she says her boots are '*nine*'?—
　　　　That's a joke between us,—
She's a foot outruns the breeze,
Killing ankles if you please,
You should see her climbing trees !
　　　　May, my pocket Venus.

In abbreviated frock
That would Mrs. Grundy shock,
　　　　Had she only seen us—
Tripping, dancing like a fay,
Playing hide and seek—some day
I should like to hide away
Altogether charming May
　　　　As my pocket Venus !

TWENTY-ONE TO-MORROW.

YOU are young ; I'm getting old,
       Cara Mia !
In the glass when I behold
Touched locks in contrasted fold,
Mine are grey, and yours are gold,
       Cara Mia.

Forty—twenty ; that 's the score,
       Cara Mia ;
Two to one,—a trifle o'er—
Why weren't you a decade more ?
Why am I not twenty-four,
       Cara Mia ?

Twice your age ! no time to say,
       ' Cara Mia ; '
Doubled years make short delay . . .
Happy thought ! after to-day
Can't again be *doubled*, eh,
       Cara Mia ?

PART II.

THE NIGHT MAIL NORTH.

(EUSTON SQUARE, 1840.)

NOW then, take your seats! for Glasgow and the
   North;
Chester!—Carlisle!—Holyhead,— and the wild Frith of
    Forth:
    "Clap on the steam and sharp's the word,
      "You men in scarlet cloth:—

    "Are there any more pas . . sengers,
    "For the Night . . Mail . . to the North!"

      Are there any more passengers?
      Yes three   but they can't get in, —
Too late, too late!   How they bellow and knock,
They might as well try to soften a rock
      As the heart of that fellow in green.

    For the Night Mail North? what ho
    (No use to struggle, you can't get thro'
      My young and lusty one—
    Whither away from the gorgeous town?

" For the lake and the stream and the heather brown,
  "And the double-barrelled gun ! "

For the Night Mail North, I say?
  You, with the eager eyes —
You with the haggard face and pale ?—

" From a ruined hearth and a starving brood,
  " A Crime and a felon's gaol ! "

For the Night Mail North, old man ?—
  Old statue of despair—
Why tug and strain at the iron gate ?
" *My daughter ! !* "

Ha ! too late, too late,
She is gone, you may safely swear ;
She has given you the slip, d'you hear ?
She has left you alone in your wrath, --
And she's off and away, with a glorious start,
To the home of her choice, with the man of her heart,
  By the Night Mail North !

       .   .   .   .

       .   .   .   .

Wh————ish, R————ush,
Wh————ish, R————ush . . .
  " What's all that hullabaloo ?
  " Keep fast the gates there--who is this
  " That insists on bursting thro' ? "

A desperate man whom none may withstand,
For look, there is something clench'd in his hand
 Tho' the bearer is ready to drop --
  He waves it wildly to and fro,
And hark ! how the crowd are shouting below --
   " Back ! "
 And back the opposing barriers go,
" *A reprieve for the Cannongate murderer, Ho !*
  " *In the Queen's name—*
   " STOP.
  " *Another has confessed the crime.*"

  Whish— rush - whish— rush . . .

 The Guard has caught the flutt'ring sheet,
Now forward and northward ! fierce and fleet,
Thro' the mist and the dark and the driving sleet,
  As if life and death were in it ;
 'Tis a splendid race ! a race against Time, —
  And a thousand to one we win it :
   Look at those flitting ghosts --
   The white-arm'd finger-posts—
If we're moving the eighth of an inch, I say,
  We're going a mile a minute !
 A mile a minute— for life or death —
Away, away ! though it catches one's breath,
 The man shall not die in his wrath :

The quivering carriages rock and reel—
Hurrah ! for the rush of the grinding steel !
The thundering crank, and the mighty wheel ! — --

Are there any more pas . . sengers
For the Night . . Mail . . to the North ?

REJECTED.

AND she is gone ! - my beauty, my sweetheart,
My first, last love – and, with her, light,
And all that has made the gladness. . . . A minute ago
She was here ; is not that the scent
Of eglantine, the wreath she wore in her hair ?
A minute ago ! but a century
Stands between Now and Then !
Then, life was divine   joy's cup sparkled up to the brim—
Hope trod upon air ; but now,
Now they are ashes and dust —
Hope and its blossoms withered out in the bud, and life
Is barren and salt and bitter as Dead Sea fruit.

. . . And yet I thought that she loved me,—
She whom I loved
With a love that was lover and brother in one,
And that craved but a word
To pour itself out at her feet   yea, body and soul,
And the spirit and every thought -
In a passionate incense of loving at her one shrine.
But she could give none in return ;
She told me the truth but now ;

Liked me, and so on (of course), as a friend ;
But for *love*— Bah ! Blind that I was —
Blind to have wooed her ; mad to suppose I had won ;
Fooled by myself to the top of my own wild bent ! . . .

Yet I never wooed her fairly !
I hadn't a chance from the first ;
For how shall he win the heart that has known him
never as lover ?—
I cut myself off from hope—
My own hand cut me off
Yea ev'n from the pitiful thought that with time,
Time and true tendance of whatsoever a man can give
The woman he worships, love had begotten love . . .

And I fancied she knew it all.
That passion like mine,
Lighting my being like flame, could not be unknown
At the shrine where its daily, hourly incense rose ;
Could not be unfelt
At the very altar from which its fire was fed.
But I understand it now ;
The veil has dropt from my eyes :
The frank young heart no shadow of love had crossed
So quick to be kind for kindness, and say the thing that
was sweet, —
The girl such a very woman—
The woman still but a girl,

So utterly trusting in friendliness, fancy free
And I, that would fain have been nearer
And dearer than friend, misconstruing all ;
The blush when I praised her songs the sigh —
The tell-tale droop of the fringèd lids —
The something that still was nought,   but which love,
Feigning its own reflection in her it loved,
Wove into proofs fate-strong,
And that blind judge,
The heart, summed up amiss. — Oh, fooled !
Fooled ! but not hers the blame ; no fault,
No speck for my sweet white lily, no hint
Of a wrong in her ;
Unless a blame be her sweetness—unless it were
Her fault to be so that I could not choose but love her ;
Oh ! unless
Those exquisite depths of blue, her eyes,
That were my heav'n, be wrongs.

  .   .   .   .   .   .

But what remains ?
Despair : a blank : an empty heart, acting false smiles,
Like flowery urns that glitter over decay.
These ; and at last (and worst that mocking Time
Can do to humble proud humanity,)
Mean ' resignation,' base ' contentment,' tame
Dull acquiescence in the thing that is, and loss
Even of the consolation of great woe. . .

For misery cuts like a sharp sword, yet slayeth not --
   And memory's stabs grow blunt.
     O for a death
In some brave battle-shock, where steel meets steel, and
no man turns—
     To dash out life
  Against some giant wrong-doer of the world,
  Striking one gallant stroke. . . .
       But death
 Comes not at call, even to the tortured wretch
   Praying for his advent :
    I shall live—
Live to act out to the last act my part in destiny,
 Nor like a coward turn my back on fate.
  Duty must teach existence to endure. . . .
 'Tis nothing--but one broken heart the more.

THE ROSE OF ETTRICK.

FULL fresh and fair thy wreath to-day,
    Old Newark's ivied tower ;
Still blooms the leaf and buds the spray
    In Yarrow's birchen bower ;
By Ettrick-bank the soft sweet mays
    Their whites and crimsons jostle—
            Ah !
But softer, sweeter seems to me
The bloom thy cheek wears changefully,
        Sweet Mary Russell :
And nothing half so fresh and fair
Draws loving life from perfumed air.

To many a breeze your sylvan song
    Makes music, Lindan beeches,
Full many a streamlet trills along,
    Bright Tweed, thy pebbly reaches ;
And here the lark sings loud and clear,
    There fluteth low the throstle—
            Ah !
But clearer comes thy voice to me
And tenderer thy minstrelsy,
        Sweet Mary Russell :

                                    E

For that has still a touch love-lorn,
A charm of winds nor waters born.

And winter woods shall mourn their frost,
  All leaf snow-burial craving ;
The thrush's tuneful voice is lost
  In the hoarse torrent's raving ;
And fairest things must fade, and lie
  At last on death's cold tressle . . .
            Ah !
But, Beautiful, *thou* shalt not die—
I give thee immortality,
        Sweet Mary Russell !
These simple flow'rs such merit claim,
Fadeless as love, *immortelles* is their name.

THE PICTURE GALLERY.

THERE is a dim, long gallery in the brain,
 Thick woof'd, and hung with pictures of the past :
A vista'd gallery of many doors
And haunting aisles, guarded by voiceless things
That whisper not nor murmur 'twixt their wings
But sleep : sustaining each th' appointed badge
Of office, chainwise, hardly to be waked
And yielding up the Secret of the Key
But to the exact pass and countersign.
 These are the Chambers of the Imagery ;
Sealed, symbol-wrought about the walls, and scroll'd
With portents, ghostly, not to be rehearsed.
Still treasure-houses are they, in the which
Are stored life's photographs, slide over slide ;
Shapes foul and beautiful—most strange · but true :
Precisely accurate from the mystic glass
Of the soul's camera.
   These with fancy forms,
And airy nothings of the inner world,
That were but are not ; gender'd of a sleep,
And lost with waking, like the ice-white ferns
Struck by the sceptre of the feathery frost.

So, when the heart of man is faint within,
Or anguish-wrung, or smitten by remorse,
There comes to him a thought, linked with a sign—
A look, a tone, a little golden curl,
The veriest mote, perchance, that swims the beam
Insensuous—but a hint of something gone—
Comes silently to those dim doors, and knocks ;
And he that has the office wakes at once
And strikes the portal of his treasure-house
And yields up all.   Each secret of his charge,
Th' estranged familiars of the buried past,
They start to sight !   From frame and tapestry,
Each shadowy close, each nook gives up its dead,—
From the still earth their voices cry to us,—
Th' impalpable air takes form, and of the tomb
Come forth the lovely, call us by our names
With lisping accent, and that last fond look—
The last of death and first of life—that told
The Giver had ta'en back his gift. . . .

                              They bring
Gleams on their wings of childhood, misty May,
Bright June, with him, the man of our own heart,
The one twin soul we thought to knit to ours
For ever : gone !——and at the word
As from the fountains of the deep gush forth
Th' imprisoned floods of memory ; eddying sweep

Time's turbid waves, each with his jewelled freight
Of withered sweets— dead hopes, dead joys—rise up
To the heart's brim, o'erflow, and blurr out all, —
Save one loved face, like a familiar star
Resting upon the dark, with angel eyes
And sweeping hair that shadow'd all our birth.

Vivid they stand, as parted yesterday,—
The rose is on the cheek, the husht lips move,—
Form, feature, bearing, nature-printed each ;
Yea to that woman of the hollow heart
And lovely lying brow and Judas smile—
The clear cold smile that froze along the lip—
Cut to the icy life ! . . .

So rest they, haunters of the bodiless past ;
Of the Soul's Picture Gallery locked and barred
And guarded by a spell, nor summoned thence
But by a sign potential, or till he,
The mighty solver of all mysteries,
That holds the Master-key, shall unlock all.

A SLIDE.

WHO'LL climb with me the Jungfrau height?
     Look how she sleeps in the evening light,
All rosy tinted with breast aglow—
That's where the sunset has touched the snow—
And then again on the under slope,
     (Only a soft white slope, fond lover!)
White as wool and softer than down,
Swan's-down, thistle-down, softer and smoother ·
'Twould be brave and bright in the sunset light
     To slide like a snow-wreath over?

Yes, white and soft, soft and white,
Is the breast of my fair Jungfrau to-night!
A slide in her arms would be brave, I trow,—
No need to stop to take breath, you know,
For a couple of thousand feet, or so—
And the thread-like crack showing out below
(Just a cleft with dark water wand'ring thro'—
     Your mountain brook was ever a rover ··)
Is deepish, they say, but not very wide,—
A chamois might spring to the other side,
     Or—slip like a snow-wreath over?

'PINCHER.'

FAREWELL—sleep soft ! whilst over mosses grow,
   Kindest of all thy race was ever seen ;
Some tears are thine, some drops of long adieu
   From hearts where still thy memory shall be green.

Farewell !—but oh ! how often didst thou lay
   A soft head and brown eyes upon my breast,
Nestling, and sighing deep, as if to say
   ' I love, I love you—master, think the rest ! '

Companion both and terror of my gun,
   Who all inapt, yet ardent for the chase,
Plung'd in the crackling marsh when snipe was down,
   Spurr'd by ambitions alien to thy race ;

Or else, when bluebells rang thro' woods of May
   Girt by the winding stream where alders nod,
How wouldst thou drive th' amphibious foe to bay
   Dripping and panting like some river-god ! . . . .

Farewell ! farewell ! and yet one last caress,
   Old comrade - friend— for truer ne'er can be :
Whose faults were only virtues in excess,
   Whose virtues faultless—there's a star for thee !

TO A LADY WITH A RING.

SWEET Valentine, dear lady mine,
　　Love lays an offering at your shrine—
Yet mete not by this span of gold
That which would reach thro' years untold,
Would burn when life itself is cold.
Not with the dazzling fitful gleam
That gilds the stripling's fever-dream
(For love --the dream-love of the boy—
Is but a glittering summer toy)—
But with the strong and steady glow,
But with the deep and tender flow,
That a man's heart alone can know,
Pouring his soul out at her feet
Whose smile can make all dark things sweet . . .
Love undivided close and dear
With ready arm to guide and cheer,
His breast her shield from every fear :
Love changeless still, where change is rife,
Thro' storm and calm, thro' peace and strife,
For grief for joy, for death for life !
Love breathed in one soft whisper—wife.

OUTSIDE.

JUST a gleam thro' the darkness,
　The lift of two eyes from a book—
　　A glance . . . but some glances are heaven,
　　To such eyes 'tis given
To make Paradise in a look.

Just a face in the lamp-light,
A hand and some glittering hair—
　　But hearts have been broken, it's said,
　　And white steel stained red,
For faces less faultlessly fair.

Just a girl in her beauty,
Her glory of freshness and youth. . . .
　　But what has earth better to sigh for,
　　To live for, to die for,
Than innocence, beauty, and —Ruth?

REQUIESCAT IN PACE.[1]

IN MEMORIAM, THOMAS PEABODY.

WE send him home.
   England sends home her son—*her* son, for he
Is yours, and ye our first-born—sends him home,
As nations send the men they honour most,
In pride and state and pomp of splendid death.

   We send him home :
The land he loved to his own loving land :
The loan to the lender : and we add thereto
A royal usury—a people's tears.

   We send him home,—
The kindly heart, the simple gentleman,—
And sending say, 'This message spans the gulf
We stretch across, as with a fleshly arm,
And our own flesh (oh, never doubt) will clasp
The hand of brotherhood with strong right hand. . .
Wipe out the past.   All but the old kind years,
Before an oft-regretted harshness snapt

---

[1] Published in the *Standard*, on the day Peabody's remains were sent back
to America in an English ship of war.

The filial link ; the years when England still
Was " home " to far-off hearths, and saw with pride
Her Titan offspring towering into strength. . . .'

   Wipe out the past : the wrongs, the unnatural
      strife -
And the red blood that English hands have pour'd
From English veins. War is a curse but war
Betwixt one race, one kindred, doubly cursed.
   What gain in war ? No gain, but loss of much,
Of life, of treasure : gain of honour, then ?
The weaker falls what honour to the strong ?—
Oh, war, what honour hast thou ? Honour none. . .
But war treads down the blossoming rose of peace,
With iron heel stamps out the smould'ring sparks
Of spiritual fire, and the strugglings faint
Of poor blind dumb humanity for light.

   We send him home
Who showed a better way. With good, not ill,
He nobly conquered ; and where darkness reigned
Amidst the abodes of night, made day himself
Illumined by the brightness that he gave.
   He taught us Love ; lay we the theme to heart,
Prelude alike and close of all that is :
And whilst with stooping flag and muffled march,
The great ship bears the lowly to his rest ;

Whilst twice ten thousand brazen lips ring woe,
And thousand thousand hearts re-echo it ;
Yea, whilst the funeral peal is thundering forth
Ev'n from the black cannon-mouths agape for war—
Join we our hands above the gracious dead,
And, mingling tears in one long sorrow, swear
To write this epitaph above him—PEACE.

'DREI BITTEN.'

BLUE flow'r to true love dear
By haunted fountain drips,
Lend me thy lips.
That I may whisper, whisper in His ear.

Lonely, my star of night,
Lovely pale star that lies
Trembling as twilight dies,
Give me thine eyes
That He may look up into mine for light.

And, oh, ye birds of wood !
And vocal fields and plain,
Hymning soft praise in vain
For me answering not again,
Teach me your strain—
I too would sing for ever, Love is good.

FROM HOLYHEAD TO DUBLIN.

WHISTLE away, my beauty, whistle away!
　　Stretch your big lungs to it, do—
Here's a gale that can sing, if you can play,
　　And fifty miles of tumbling blue
(Except where the froth comes churning thro')
　　Between us and Dublin Bay,—
And not a keel but yours one may swear
　　Will cut it to-day. . . .

' Ho! it's merry to play on a pipe of steel
　　The tune that the surges sing;
Ho! it's merry to drive with a whirling wheel
　　When the heaving billows swing:
When the light has gone out in the sulphur skies
Save the flying flash that flickers and dies—
When the storm drum is up, and the mast is low,
'Tis merry, 'tis merry—ho ho! ho ho!—
　　To dance with the Tempest King. —
No stately minuet soft and slow,
But a gallop the pace the whirlwinds go
　　To the sweep of the hurricane's wing,—
And the surge that swells and the storms that blow,
The whistling scud and the driving snow

And the wild wave thundering to and fro,
Come dance to the chorus—ho ho ! ho ho !
And the iron engines ring . . . . '

.   .   .   .   .   .

Is that your idea of music, old girl ? -
Well it sounds to me like Dutch :
Your voice is a trifle hoarse, and those powdering wheels
That make such a mess of the Channel don't mend it much,
But I take your meaning, my lass,
Tho' I'll not pretend to sing
We care as much for the gale, you and I,
As that broad white herring-gull slanting by,
And that seems to be keeping us company,
As it were ' for the love of the thing ? '
That's about what you're saying, I reckon, and true for
you :
We like a brush now and then with these bullying seas ;
We can't stop to curtsey, you know,
And we're rather stiff in the bow —
So we just *walk thro' them*, by way of a friendly squeeze.

There's one cresting up there, right over the hurricane deck
Ahead of us now,
With a mane like the father of all sea-serpents —*slick !*
We're thro' it or under, it's no matter how,—
But here's one behind it, my girl, you'd be sorry to miss
Keep your head straight

A ' damper ' may happen to take your hair out of curl—
Slick !—hiss—s. . . .
Bravely done ! . . . never stagger and shake—
What's a ton of green sea more or less
When it all rolls off before it gets to the grate ?
Keep the powder dry, and Old King Coal for a pinch —
' Wallsend best,' that's the thing,—
There's nothing like coal and a hundred pounds pressure
the inch
To lick your regular rattling Atlantic swing . . .
If you want to beat water try *fire*,
Or steam, I should say,
So look to your stoking, my beauty—
And whistle away !

MODERN BABYLON.

(EXTRACTS.)

THE END?

WHAT shall I write ? – for I feel a power within
    To drive my thought like a sword thro' the
twisted mail
And the adamant scales of a monster shame and sin,
  And the might against right that has made the world
  grow pale.

What is his name ? where does he make himself strong ?
  That the swift-wing'd steel may pierce, ev'n to the
  confines of hell –
In the unpreach'd realms of the curse, deadened to sense
  of wrong,
  Where the fair Christ-light and shadow of the Rock
  never fell ?

With all that is blind and heathen and unbaptised,—
  Or here– in a land full of churches, with grace at de-
  sire, –
Where knowledge is sought as a ruby, and virtue prized,
  And the red cross flames from turret and mast like a
  fire ?

F

Here—here, in this modern Babylon, unfallen yet,
  With its thousand spires and myriad flags unfurl'd,
Whose veins overflow with their wealth of sea-gather'd
    freight,
  Whose heart is beating the mighty pulse of the world.—

This Crœsus of nations, this portent under the sky,
  Blazing with all that is richest of genius and gold,—
It is here that Dagon has set himself up on high—
  Here is his temple, here his impregnable hold.

Here, within sight of God's church, and people, and
    priests,
  Are his altars—the styes, the pestilent slime-pits, where
    men
Made in the IMAGE, transformed to the likeness of beasts,
  Wallow and fester and tear like swine in their den.

Come, Christian gentlemen ! Christian matron and maid !
  Of this fair England of ours, and claim if you can
That nameless abhorrence in rags and infamy clad,
  Once a woman, as Sister—this bestial horror, as Man—

These gin-hells as home . . . . Shame ! shame on thee,
    City of dens !—
  Thy rich are so rich, thy poor so perniciously poor :
Shameful and shameless I know that thou art, but thy sins
  Shall be laid like a plague-spotted corpse at the nation's
    door.

For these are the hot-beds of fever, the pestilence breath ;
  Here scrofula lurks and cholera stands at the gate ;
The portal is narrow and chill, but hungry as death,
  And beauty and riches and pomp and pride shall go in
    thereat.

And one day cometh a Cry,—an upsurging out of the
    clay—
And a man shall arise and smite the land with his rod,—
And the beasts shall come forth, swarm over, and slay,
    and slay,
  And the leprous city be cleansed in a Jordan of
    blood. . . .

AND AFTER?

What shall I write ? O Father of Light, give me light—
  Some light to perceive the aim and the end of life ;
More light, thou Fountain, to see the close of the fight,
  Love for hate, joy for sorrow, the rest after strife.

Not the 'rest' of the schoolman—his heav'n—not that,
    I know—
  No cloud-kissing, psalm-singing, passionless bliss,—
A living death in a dead-alive life— not so,
  Better the throb and the passionate strain of this :

Better this pulsating span with its agony-sweat—
  Hell's pain—than an age of such objectless ease :
For so were the struggle wasted--the victory won, a
    defeat—
  And the war-blade forged for the sheath of eternal
    peace.

Is not a man as a sword, picked from the dust,
  To be ground and polished and set to the Master's
    hand?
And tried in the furnace—for what ? everlasting rust ?—
  O for battle, swift battle, with wrong to the utmost
    end ?

Is a life-long action to prelude a death-long sloth ?
  Is the race-horse trained like a star to rot in the stall ?
Away with the cant-born lie I hold it as truth,
  Whatever, wherever, be Heav'n, it has work for all . . .

  .   .   .   .   .   .

I thank thee, O Father, thou hearest! thou givest me sight:
  Weak sight—but a gleam, but a glimpse of the mighty
    plan ;
My soul like a dawn-waken'd flow'r opens out to the light,
  And thought blossoms forth in the destiny dream of man.

I see far back, thro' the years of the long-ago,
  A lifeless chaos, a God with a cloud-wrapp'd face :
Reach forward, my thought—look up, sweep the mists
    from thy brow —
  Behold a cosmos, a Christ-lit glory in space !

Behold, as engrained with a pencil of light on the earth,
  Brush'd thro' the sea's green, the blue of the sky,
The purpose eternal, creative, ruling their birth,
  That shall *not* be changed, nor blotted out when they
    die, —

PROGRESS : A progress of all things under the sun,
  To perfection : of things that have life, great and small;
An infinite progress of endless existence begun,
  And man—man's soul and spirit and mind—before all.

Not thro' this orb alone, this glitt'ring atom in space,
　But onwards thro' sphere over sphere, exhausting the
　　uses of each,
Going from strength unto strength, up to the holiest place,
　Where Heaven is in sight—the Heaven of heavens
　　within reach.

Progress untold, unmeted by system and line,
　Thro' centuries past and ages yet for to come—
' I have said, ye are Gods,' the temples of Love divine—
　Be strong, be loving, O Gods! progress to your
　　home . . . .

I see far back, thro' the mists of the long-ago,
　A pulseless, lifeless, loveless, chaos of slime —
Leap forward, my thought, with pinions strengthened
　　anew,—
　Behold the cosmos, the finished wonder of time—

The Phœnix of worlds ! and she needs neither any sun,
　Nor beauty of stars, nor the silver shining of night,
Nor splendour, nor glory, nor joys evermore begun—
　For God-the-Life is her joy, God-the-Love is her light.

TO FREDERICK LOCKER.[1]

DEAR LOCKER! whom I knew unknown, but now
 Known wheresoe'er rhyme runs or critics carp,—
 None strikes a clearer, more melodious harp
   Than thou.

Thine is the spell that charms alike the sage,
 Craving repose for wearied brain and eye,
 And the fair child ling'ring her play-hour by
   Thy page.

No vulgar lures, no tinsel arts are thine
 To gild the common coarseness of the herd
 Still be thyself, unblamed in thought or word,
   And shine.

And for the lustre of thy name I hold
 Twice dear, old friend, this gleaned and garner'd
  sheaf,
 Which thence shall gain one doubly-treasured leaf
   Of gold.

[1] Dedication to ' The Muses of Mayfair.'

THE SEA'S BRIDE.

ADA dreams by the sea-beach
   (How far out the ripples reach !),
      She is very sweet ;
Comes a wave with opal lips,
Murmuring of shells and ships,
      Kissing Ada's feet.

Ada sleeps by the sea-beach.
(How close up the ripples reach—
      Will they never turn ?)
Phosphor lamps begin to shine
Glance and glow the coraline,
Till the liquid lengths of brine
      Into flashes burn.

Ada wakes by the sea-beach,
Round and round the deep waves reach,
      Sways the eddying tide,
Clasps and clings the amber weed ;
Prays the maiden - she has need,
      'Mid the waters wide.

Sea, thine arms are very soft ;
Wave, thy kisses wake not oft ;
Rock her, billow, soft and slow ;
Surge, sing to her light and low,
        Cheer thy bonny bride.

A DAISY CHAIN.

THE white rose decks the breast of May,
　　The red rose smiles in June,
Yet autumn chills and winter kills
　　And leaves their stems alone;
Ah, swiftly dies the garden's pride
　　Whose sleep no waking knows,—
But my love she is the daisy
　　That all the long year grows.

The early woods are gay with green,
　　The fields are prankt with gold,
But fair must fade and green be greyed,
　　Before the year is old ;
The blue-bell hangs her shining head,
　　No more the oxlip blows,—
But my love she is the daisy
　　That all the long year grows.

Still deck, wild woods, your mantle green,
　　All meads bright jewels wear,
Let show'rs of Spring fresh violets bring
　　And sweetness load the air ;
Whilst summer boasts her roses red
　　And March her scented snows,—
My love be still the daisy,
　　And my heart whereon she grows.

ENGLISH SUTTEE.

H O, Sceva ! -deck the chamber
    Flash the wild revel up !
Till the fiery goblet sparkles
   And fury crowns the cup :
Wreathe, wreathe the bridal chaplet,
   The sacred rights proclaim --
To-night another victim
   Shall come to thee in flame.
Th' appointed victim waits thee ! . .
   Let music fling its spell,
Whilst husht lips murmur pleasure,
   And answ'ring whispers thrill ;
Whilst eyes with love are lighting
   And tender glances meet,
And the dizzy valse flies faster
   To the sweep of silken feet :
In the flush of airy triumph
   She comes ! a bride elect--
A gleam of gauzy splendour,
   A sacrifice full-deckt.

And lo ! the altar waiting—
   Already round her crowd

The ministers of torture,
 The weavers of her shroud :
They press . . . .
  O God ! *the fire !* ———
 Too late they shriek her name—
Wild thro' the frenzied tumult
 She flies, a living flame.
Away ! in vain all succour ;
 In vain the passionate strife
Of the fond hearts that clasp her,
 Life scorning for her life,—
The red king's arms are round her,
 He does his work right well :
Lover, take up thy Beauty —
 What lies there ? Canst thou tell ?

A bride ? ay, for thee, lovely,
 A bridegroom truly comes,
With pomp of sable pageant
 In pride of nodding plumes ;
The solemn priest stands ready,
 The wedding guests are there,
But hearts with grief are breaking,
 And one shall wed — despair. . . .
And long for thee shall sorrow
 Sit mute at hearth and hall,

For thee the lip shall tremble
   The blinding tear shall fall ;
And the fresh spring shall come over,
   And the flowers with the summer's breath,
But thou shalt know no spring-time,
   Whose bridal fere was Death.

THE TWO CHAMPIONS.

Frowning they stood, the Lords of Night and Day,—
Betwixt them roll'd an orb.

I SAW an armèd champion ride
    Slow toward the West ;
With a crimson flush of wavering light
    On his crest :
His visor was up, and his helmeting
    Blazed like a dome of gold ;—
A sun-red shield on his breast he bore,
And a blood-red sun shone evermore
    On his buckler manifold.

Stood purple-smit his giant frame ;
The summer lightnings went and came ;
Outstream'd his hair, like yellow flame—
    Outstream'd in wavelets free :
In shining folds over dingle and hill
The flood of silken lustre fell,
And slowly trailed along the vale,
And lightly brush'd the upland pale,
    And swept across the sea !
It was a noble sight I trow,
That warrior with his burning brow

So red from spur to plume,—
So splendid in his stately pace —
As if a God had set his face
Towards some far-off resting-place,
 And left a world to gloom.

  . . . . .

Then saw I, rising slowly up
 Behind the Eastern low,
A champion clad in silver mail,
And breast and brow were ghastly pale
 Even as Atlas snow.
And all the pure, crisp, icy world
 Flash'd back the glittering wonder ;
And look'd up at the great white face
 That cleft the dark asunder.

His pennon flew like a thunder-cloud
(When the angry winds are piping loud
 From deep to deep)
Above the warrior's helmèd head
 In billowy sweep :
His uttermost form in the shadowing South
Hung cloud-fringed to the view ;
  Azure and black
  Were his corslet and jack,
And his plume the stars shone thro'. —

There liveth none might cope with him
    Save he of the burning brow. . . .

And ever those two champions ride
    In solemn silence past :
And neither knight may meet his foe
    The whiles the world shall last.

IN A GONDOLA.

DARK, it is dark ! The stars have all gone out,
  There is no moon with watery smiles to flout
  The cold smile rippling round a colder mouth,
  That parches not my thirsty soul with drouth
  Like a red lip, left in the rich South.

Dark, it is dark ! There is no light at all,
Except with the long oar-blade's rise and fall,—
  Except the phosphor flashes of the brine
  And the quick light of eyes that gleam in mine,
  But wake no fires, Guinevra, as did thine.

Dark, it is dark—the darkness of black night,—
Darkness of skies, and all that should be bright ;
  Darkness of waves, where the black shores begin,
  A darkness wrapping one fair child of sin,
  Darkness of all without—and all within.

G

FROM 'THE THREAD OF LIFE.'

EXTRACT.

.   .   .   .   .   .

UNSEARCHABLE depths of a Mother's heart !
  Unfathom'd ocean by line or chart !
Can you gauge me, I say, one thousandth part
    Of the feelings that stir within it ?
What a freight that little Existence bears
Of pallid smiles and tremulous tears,
Of joys never breathed into mortal ears,
Griefs that the callous world never hears,
Suff'ring that only the more endears,
And love, that would reach into endless years,
    Snuff'd out, it may be, in a minute ! . . .

Would you look on a mother in all her pride ?
Her radiant, dazzling, glorious pride ?
Then seek yon garret - leaden-eyed -
And thrust the mould'ring panel aside—
    The door that has nothing to lock it
And the walls are tatter'd, and damp, and drear,
And the light has a quivering gleam, like fear,
For the hand of Sickness is heavy here,
    And the lamp burns low in the socket.

'Mid rags, and want, and misery, piled,
A woman is watching her stricken child,
With a love so tender, a look so mild,
That the little suff'ring babe has smiled
    A smile that is strangely fair !—
And lo ! in that chamber, poverty-dyed,
A mother in all her dazzling pride—
    A glorious mother is there !

And the child is squalid, and puny, and thin, —
But hush hush your voice as you enter in !
Nor dare to despise, lest a deadly sin
    On your soul rest unforgiven ; –
Perchance, oh scornful and worldly-wise,
A SHAKESPEARE dreams in those thoughtful
  eyes —
A NEWTON looks out at the starry skies—
Or a 'prison'd angel in calm surprise
    Looks back to its Heaven !

THE BOAT RACE.

THERE'S a living thread that goes winding, winding,
 Tortuous rather, but easy of finding,
   Creep and crawl
   By paling and wall—
  Very much like a dust-dry snake—
 From Hyde Park Corner right out to Mortlake ;
   Crawl and creep
   By level and steep,
From Putney Bridge back again to Eastcheap,—
   Horse and man,
   Waggon and van,
  Tramping along since the day began—
 Rollicking, rumbling, and rolling apace,
With their heads all one way like a shoal of dace ;
   And beauty and grace,
   The lofty and base,
   Silk, satins, and lace,
   And the evil in case,
  Seem within an ace of a general embrace—
 Jog-trotting behind the Lord Mayor with his mace —
   As if the whole place
   Had set its whole face
  Towards the Oxford and Cambridge Race.

  . . . . . .

Has any one seen some grand, fleet horse
At the starting-post of an Epsom course,
With nostril spread and chest expanding,
But like a graven image standing,
Waiting a touch to start into life
And spurn the earth in the flying strife ;
Whilst around, with restless eddying pace,
Frolic the froth and foam of the race ?—
   So side by side
   Like shadows they glide,
Two streaks of blue just breasting the tide,
Whilst a thousand oars are glitt'ring wide,
   Flash'd in the morning beam,—
And so, as when waked to sudden speed
Darts from the throng the flying steed,
   They darted up the stream.

   With a rush and a bound,
   And a surging sound,
From the arches below and the boats around,
And the background of everything wooden and steel
  That's driven by oar, sail, paddle, or wheel,
   Striving and tearing,
   And puffing and swearing,
With the huge live swarm that their decks are bearing,
  A sound from bridge and river and shore,
  That gathers into a human roar. —

'*Cambridge! Cambridge!*'—'*Now, Oxford, now!*'
    Betwixt the crews
    There isn't a pin to choose—
Not so much as the turn of a 'feather'—
    The Cambridge eight
    Have muscle and weight,
But the dark blue blades fall sharp and straight,
As the hammer of Thor on the anvil of fate,
    So wholly they pull together.

    And they pull with a will! . . . .
    Row, Cambridge, row,
They're going two lengths to your one, you know—
    The Oxford have got the start,—
    Out and in—at a single dash—
    Flash and feather, feather and flash,
    Without a jerk or an effort or splash
It's a stroke that will break your heart. . . .
A wonderful stroke! but a *leetle* too fast?
    Forty-four to the minute at least;
For five or six years it's been all your own way,
But you've got your work cut out to-day,
    Give them the Cambridge swing, I say,
The grand old stroke, with its sweep and sway,
And send her along!—never mind the spray—
    It's a mercy the pace can't last. . . .
They never can 'stay'? tho' the Turn is in sight. . .

Ha, now she lifts !—row, row ! . . .
      But in spite
Of the killing pace, and the stroke of might,
In spite of bone and muscle and height,
On flies the dark blue like a flash of blue light,
    And the river froths like yeast. . . .

    ' Oxford, Oxford ! she wins, she wins '——
Well, you've won ' the toss,' you see,
      Whilst the Cantabs must fetch
       Their boats thro' a stretch
    That's as lumpy and cross as may be ;
And the men are too big, and the boat's too small,
For a rushing tide and a racing squall —
But look ! by the bridge, a haven for all —
    And Cambridge may win if she can ; —
And the squall's gone down and the froth is past,
And you'll find it's the ' pace that kills ' at last —
    You must *pull*, do you understand ? —
Put your backs into it   now or never —
Jam home your feet whilst the clench'd oars quiver,
For over the gold of the gleaming river
They're passing you, hand over hand :
      And a thousand cheers
      Ring in their ears —
The muscles stand out on their arms like cords,
    Brows knit and teeth close set,—

And bone and weight are beginning to tell,
And the swingeing stroke that the Cam knows well
    Will lick you yet. . . .
Cambridge ! Cambridge ! again—bravo—
Splendidly pulled—now, Trinity, now—
    Now let the oars sweep—
    Now, whilst the shouts rise,
    And the white foam flies,
And the stretch'd boat seems to leap !
Stick to it, boys, for the bonny light blue . . .

And the turquoise silk dasht with the spray
    Steals forward now :
    Rowed, rowed of all ! . . .
      . . . But what ails the crew ?—
What ails the strong arms, unused to wax dull ?
And the light boat trails like a wounded gull . . . ?

   .   .   .   .   .   .

    Swamped ! swamped, by heaven ;
      Beat, in mid fight,
      With the goal in sight,
        As they were gaining fast —
        Row, Cambridge, row !
Swamped, while the great crowd roared,
      Wash over wash it poured
      Inch by inch
      Does a man flinch ?

Row, Cambridge, row !—
Stick to it to the last —
Over the brown waves' crest
Only the oarsmen's breast,
Yet, Cambridge, row ;
One gallant stroke, pulled all altogether —
One more ! . . . and a long flash in the dark river,
And the dark blue shoots past.

WITH THE HORSE 'WHITE-MIST.'[1]

THE sequel of to-day dissevers all
    This fellowship of straight riders, and hard men
To hounds—the flyers of the hunt. . . .
                                    I think
That we shall never more in days to come
Hold cheery talk of hounds and horses (each
Praising his own the most)— shall steal away
Through brake and coppice-wood, or side by side
Breast the sharp bullfinch and deep-holding dyke,
Sweep through the uplands, skim the vale below,
And leave the land behind us like a dream.

    Farewell to all ! to the brave sport I loved—
Though Paget sware that I should ride again—
But yet I think I shall not ; I have done :
My hunt is hunted : I have skimm'd the cream,
The blossom of the seasons, and no more
For me shall gallant Scott have cause for wrath,
Or injured Springwheet mourn his wasted crops.

[1] Lines sent with a favourite horse to the late Charles Buxton, M.P., the most genial and charming of companions, and one of the straightest riders to hounds, on the occasion of author giving up hunting owing to an accident in the hunting-field.

Now, therefore, take my horse, which was my pride
For still thou know'st he bore me like a man—
And wheel him not, nor plunge him in the mere,
But set him straight and give his head the rein,
And he shall bear thee lightly to the front,
Swifter than wind, and stout as truest steel,
And none shall rob thee of thy pride of place.

CRESCENT?

OR THE AGE OF POETRY.

FROM ' PRELUDE.'

THERE are lack-lustre eyes, purblind and blear,
    Which at high noon see all things in eclipse ;
There are dull adder ears that only hear
    Nature's file-scrapings ; men with blistered lips . . .
That spit their poison round, and make a noise
    Quite disproportioned to such feeble folks,—
Great trumpet-blowings, chorusing themselves,—
    And each encoring each, as two small frogs
Grown bold by darkness and applauding elves
    Fill a whole marsh with their obstreperous croaks. . . .

And so croak on, small men ! and spit your spite—
    You cannot croak the sun to hide his day,
Nor hatch a poison to unsilver night,
    Nor frown the hawthorn from the breast of May,—
Nor make sweet Mother Nature veil her charms
    Because you see no beauty in her face—
But evermore she opens wide her arms,
    To clasp the sons of song in her beloved embrace.

I.

' The Age of poetry is past : its pride,
 Blossom and bud and gem, wither'd and sear.—
It droop'd with loss of plume and wave of steel,—
   It paled in Love's pale beam ;
         It died
   On chivalry's splintered spear. . .'

Again—' The king-roll of the bards is sealed ;
The thrones complete, up to the end of time :
The hands that only could the sceptre wield
      Were of the poets' prime.
The harp those masters smote is now unstrung,' . . .
Ay, as the rain-wreath ! Heav'n's full-bended bow,
Scatt'ring its shafts of light on sullen mists below,
Unstrung as nerves that rush on level steel.

        .   .   .   .   .   .

Oh, false, that poetry is dead ! the wreath
Each human thing draws round it lives and blooms :
A poetry is born with every birth,
Love lit, love tended, crowned with parting breath,—
A song of life, a coronac of death —
Some hand still plants the violet on our tombs ? . . .

Earth, ocean, air, beloved Sisterhood,
Are ye too dead—your poems pass'd away?
The forest concord, the melodious vale?
Is there no harmony of winds by day —
No nightly music of the tinkling rill?
Does sunset stint his vespers, ruby-lit,
Or morn her orisons of beaded dew?
Where is the noise of rain among the leaves,
And where the silence of the falling snow?
The hush of peaks, the deep sea's whisp'ring flow?
   Are these no more? . . .

  From yonder hazel glen
I hear the voice of water, like a spell,
  Faint, dreamy; morning moves
Her leaves on a west wind, and thro' the tassel'd fir,
Over the dewy incense-breathing stir,
   There comes a sound of doves:
April's preluding to the sweet May airs,
Spring's welcome to her first-born—Hark! she calls!
From oxlip banks her tiny trumpets blow;
A peal of bells from the blue underwood
   Ring summer: even so.

 . . . . . .

False, false, that song is dead! all these
Live in their place, and beautify their hour!
Each strikes his poem on the soul of man—

Yea, and that soul still vibrates to the pow'r :
A grand Æolian, harping life and death,
Sweet as of yore, and waked by lightest breath
To voiceless melody ; strains felt, not sung ;
Th' unutter'd poetries that make men gods.
The lone, strong fight for Fame fought out and won,
The wrestlings of proud hearts temptation-wrung,
The life-long love of right and deathless hate of wrong,
Helpings of helplessness and scorn of odds.

   .   .   .   .   .   .

II.

'Yea, but '—they say   'we ask some sensuous note :
Some hint of the old strength   of Power, not here :
The poetry struck out from glinting steel
With clash of knightly arms and trumpet peal,
The poetry that Beauty   matchless then —
Inspired in songs of bards and hearts of men,
When fairest love was prize of sharpest spear. . .

A fatal prize, bought with so dear a coin —
A ghastly love, whose bridal bow'r is death –
An un-sexed beauty, that must twine its brows
     With such a ruddy wreath !
But matchless ? No - unless unmatch'd as grows

The wild hedge-thorn beside the grafted rose,—
The scentless by the perfumed, crude by ripe,—
As a green waste by flowering Eden shows.

Fairer our forms, from nature's latest touch,
From culture fine and intellectual growth—
Fair with mind-beauty, and the spiritual life
Graft on a perfect stem of loveliest earth :
A beauty blossoming in gentle deeds,
By modest truth and sweet domestic grace :
By every thought-lit star Refinement sets
In the soft heaven of a woman's face.
By freer love ; by pure speech, doubly free ;
By true ambitions purged of civil broil ;
By faith broad-based, with loftier temples crown'd ;
By fairer office and a nobler toil. . . .

　·　　　·　　　·　　　·　　　·　　　·

Believe each kind word finds an echo here,
Some biding place, some breast whereon to sleep ;
Or finding not, turns back to its own ark
As the dove turned from the unrestful deep.

　·　　　·　　　·　　　·　　　·　　　·

III.

So then, to sum up all, that it may rest
And glitter like a star on memory's sky,
As a last cadence lingers on the ear
And the last dream-look on the waking eye; —
To sum all up   the themes for modern song,
Its bards, with those before them   this remains :
We gain their loss, but cannot lose their gains. . . .

Nor are the altars whereon Song delights
To pour her loftiest strains thrown down or cold,
Nature still boasts her universal throne,
And sceptred Love his empiry of old.
These two alike, spells potent then as now,
But all things else converging to our day :
Courage more high, Religion whiter robed,
And beauty shining with supremer ray.
The book of man, the wondrous human page,
Open'd more wide, even with wid'ning times
And kindlier men,   that text for poet rage !
Wherein is set life sorrowings, hopings, fears,
Lovings and loathings blotted in with tears. . . .
    Material Power reigning like a god,
Huge, iron-crown'd, and striding half a sphere :

Keen intellect, with ever upward stroke,
Oaring new heights and fields of freer air ; --
Arms, arts, wealth, learning, each of larger sway,
And Science wing'd where Genius points the way.
But all things germin ; ampler in their age ;
Budding like Aaron's rod in Israel's sight :
All living pillars growing up to Truth ;
Shafts in the dome whose pinnacle is   Light.

THE IRON AGE.

[FROM 'CRESCENT?']

I SAW the last White Fleet show'r down their snow
    In mirrored flakes upon the Island tide,
When forth her batteries went to tournament [1]
    In pomp of plumèd pride :
    I heard their broadsides thunder
    A requiem, ere they died !
And the sea-gull swept him lightly past,
And the red cross trailed against the mast,
    And twice ten hundred pinions there
    Hung listless in the summer air.

Afar loom'd up the long, low, strengthy hulls,
The sailless war, unwav'ring their array
No warning peal their ordnance gave,
In silence, ghastly as the grave,
Without a breath, without a wave,
    They pass'd upon their way.
And nearer to the straggling foe,
Whilst his last shots came faint and slow,
    The serried crescent drew,

---

[1] In the great naval review at Spithead, before the last Pa... campaign, t'... steam and sailing fleets manœuvred separately and in opposition to... other.

'Till prow to prow,—then round they swept,—
In one long blaze their lightnings leapt,
    And darkness hid the view :
And the smoke-wreath wrapt the White-wing'd fleet,
Meet cloak !—it was their winding-sheet.

'Tis blithe in the beams of the morning sun
    To shake out the bellying sails,
When the barque rides well on the gurgling swell
    To the lift of the fresh'ning gales —
But there's POWER in the keel with the iron wheel,
    And the breeze that never fails :
'Tis blithe—'tis brave !—against wind and wave
    To sweep with a slanting wing   —
But it's *fierce* to drive thro' the driving storm
    While the whistling tempests sing,—
Whilst the quivering axles flash like flame
    And the mighty engines ring. . . .

I know the feeling   so do you—
    If you've stood on the dark'ning deck,
When the spurr'd craft goes staggering thro'
The sharp white wave that should be blue,
And the seething gulfs seem yawning in two
    Agape for the coming wreck
He knows what it means, lasht to the wheel
Of a gallant ship in her struggle and reel,

And fierce death-grapple with foam and wind,
And the tempest that roars like an angry fiend,
  When storms above and devils below
  Seem to hiss in his ears, ' let go, let go ; '
He knows what it means ! - that tingling feel,
  Crushing out the fear that would win him :
That shivering glow from head to heel,
That sets the muscles like rigid steel,
That opens the eye   that shuts the teeth
That clenches the hand, that tightens the breath,
And lets a man know for life or for death
  How much of the GOD there is in him !

PART III.

THE FIGHT FOR THE CHAMPIONSHIP.

(AS TOLD BY AN ANCIENT ALLIGATOR TO HIS
GREAT-GRANDMOTHER.)

B IG Heenan of Benicia,
　　By ninety-nine gods he swore,
That the bright belt of England
　Should grace her sons no more.
By ninety-nine he swore it,
　And named the ' fisting ' day,
' East and west and south and north,'
Said Richard Mayne, ' ride forth, ride forth,
　' And summon mine array.'

' Ride forth by heathy Hampshire,
　Of " chalk-stream-studded " dells,
And wake the beaks of Eversley
　Where gallant Kingsley dwells ;
Spur fast thro' Berkshire spinneys,
　The broad Hog's Back bestride,
And if the White Horse is scour'd
　Mount up amain and ride :
Spur, spur, I say, thro' England ! . . .'
　The word went flashing by,

Look out for Sayers and Heenan,
　Policemen—mind your eye !

Sir Richard's bold moss-troopers
　Looked out uncommon keen,
From park and plain and prairie,
　From heath and upland green ;
From Essex fens and fallows,
　From Hampshire, dale and down,
From Sussex' hundred leagues of sand,
To Shropshire's fat and flowery land,
And Cheshire's wild and wasted strand,
　And Yorkshire's heather brown ; —
And so, of course, the fight came off
　A dozen miles from Town.

Then first stept out big Heenan,
　Unmatched for breadth and length ;
And in his chest it might be guessed,
　He had unpleasant strength.
And to him went the Sayers
　That looked both small and thin,
But well each practised eye could read
The ' lion and the bull-dog ' breed,
And from each fearless stander-by
Rang out that genuine British cry,
　' *Go in, my boy,*—and win !'

And he went in—and smote him
  Through mouthpiece and through cheek ;
And Heenan smote him back again
  Into the ensuing week :
Full seven days thence he smote him,
  With one prodigious crack,
And th' undaunted Champion straight
Discerned that he was five feet eight,
  When flat upon his back :—
Whilst a great shout of laughter
  Rose from the Yankee pack.

As from the flash the bullet,
  Out sprang the Sayers then,
And dealt the huge Benician
  A vast thump on the chin ;
And thrice and four times sternly
  Drove in the shatt'ring blow ;
And thrice and four times wavered
  The herculean foe ;
And his great arms swung wildly,
  Like ship-masts to and fro.

And now no sound of laughter
  Was heard from either side,
Whilst feint, and draw, and rally,
  The cautious Bruisers tried ;

And long they sparred and counter'd
 Till Heenan sped a thrust
So fierce and quick, it swept away
Th' opposing guard like sapling spray,—
And for the second time that day
 The Champion bit the dust.

Short time lay English Sayers
 Upon the earth at length,
Short time his Yankee foeman
 Might triumph in his strength ;
Sheer from the ground he smote him
 And his soul went with the blow --
Such blow no other hand could dash --
Such blow no other arm could smash --
 The giant tottered low ;
And for a space they sponged his face,
 And thought the eye would go.

Time's up !—Again they battle ;
 Again the strokes fly free ;
But Sayers' right arm—that arm of pride—
Now dangles pow'rless by his side,
 Plain for all eyes to see ;
And thro' that long and desperate shock—
Two mortal hours on the clock—
By sheer indomitable pluck
 With his *left hand* fought he !

With his left hand he fought him,
    Though he was sore in pain, —
Full twenty times hurled backward,
    Still pressing on again !
With his left hand he fought him,
    Till each could fight no more ;
Till Sayers could scarcely strike a blow,
Till Heenan could not see his foe
Such fighting England never knew
    Upon her soil before !

They gave him of the standard
    Gold coinage of the realm,
As much as one stout guardsman
    Could carry in his helm ;
They made him an ovation
    On the Exchange hard by, -
And they may slap their pockets
    In witness if I lie.

And every soul in England
    Was glad, both high and low,
And books were voted snobbish,
    And ' gloves ' were all the go ;
And each man told the story,
    Whilst ladies' hearts would melt,
How Sayers, the British Champion,
    Did battle for the Belt.

Yet honour to the vanquished !
(If vanquished then he were)
Let the harp strike a bolder string
And the Bird of Freedom clap his wing
For the fight so free and fair.
And forge another girdle [1]
That shall belt as brave a breast
As ever sailed to English shore
From the broad lands of the West.

And when some sterner battle
Shall shake along the line,
The Lion flag of Liberty
In Freedom's cause to shine,—
To fence its ancient honour,
And guard it safe from harms,
May *two* such Champions hand in hand
Twin brethren of the Saxon land—
Be found together to withstand
A universe in arms.

---

[1] A second 'belt was presented to Heenan as a testimony of English admiration of his gallant fight,

THE PETITION.

(PROBABLE EFFECT OF HIGHER EDUCATION ON
THE SHOE-BLACK BRIGADE.)

AH ! pause a while, kind gentleman,
 Nor turn thy face away ;
There is a boon that I must ask,
 A prayer that I would pray.

Thou hast a gentle wife at home ?
 A son— perchance like me—
And children fair with golden hair
 To cling around thy knee ?

Then by their love I pray thee,
 And by their merry tone ;
By home, and all its tender joys,
 Which I have never known, ·

By all the smiles that hail thee now ;
 By every former sigh ;
By every pang that thou hast felt
 When lone, perchance, as I, –

By youth and all its blossoms bright,
By manhood's ripened fruits,
By Faith and Hope and Charity—
You'll let me clean your boots !

SONG OF LOWER-WATER.

WHEN the summer Moon was sleeping
On the Sands of Lower-Water
By the Lowest Water Margin –
At the Mark of Dead Low Water,
Came a lithe and lovely maiden,
Crinolina, Wand'ring Whiteness,
Gazing on the ebbing water—
Gazing on the gleaming river—
With her azure eyes and tender, —
On the river glancing forward,
Till the laughing Wave sprang upward,
From his throne in Lower-Water, —
Upward from his reedy hollow,
With the lily in his bosom,
With his crown of water-lilies—
Curling ev'ry dimpled ripple
As he leapt into the starlight,
As he clasped her charmed reflection
Glowing to his crystal bosom—
As he whisper'd, ' Wand'ring Whiteness,
Rest upon my crystal bosom !
Join this little water party.' . . .
Yet she spoke not, only murmured : —

I

Down into the water stept she,
Lowest Water—Dead Low Water—
Down into the wavering river,
Like a red deer in the sunset—
Like a ripe leaf in the autumn :
From her lips, as rose-buds snow-filled,
Came a soft and dreamy music,
Softer than the breath of summer,
Softer than the murm'ring river,
Than the cooing of Cushawa,—
Sighs that melted as the snows melt,
Silently and sweetly melted ;
Sounds that mingled with the crisping
Foam upon the billow resting :

Still she spoke not, only murmured.

From the forest shade primeval,
Piggey-Wiggey looked out at her ;
He the most Successful Squeaker—
He the very Youthful Porker—
He the Everlasting Grunter—
Gazed upon her there, and wondered !
With his nose out, Rokey-pokey—
And his tail up, Curley-wurley—
Wondered what could be the matter,

Wondered what the girl was up to—
What the deuce her little game was. . . .

And she floated down the river,
Like a water-'witch'd Ophelia. . . .
FOR HER CRINOLINE SUSTAINED HER.

HOW WE GOT TO THE BRIGHTON REVIEW.

OH ! Brighton's the place
For a beautiful face,
And a figure that daintily made is ;
And as far as I know
There's none other can show
At the right time of year—say November or so—
Such lots of bewitching young ladies.

Such blows on the Down !
Such lounges thro' Town !
Such a crush at Parade and Pavilion !
Such beaches below
(Where people don't go),
Such bathing ! Such dressing,—past Madame Tussaud !
No wonder it catches the million !

For bustle and breeze
And a sniff of salt seas,
Oh, Brighton's the place ! not a doubt of it ;—
But instead of post-chaise
Or padded *coupés,*

If you had to get there *à l'excursionnaise* -
I think you'd be glad to keep out of it !

(CHORUS OF PASSENGERS.)

With their slap dash, crack crash,
And here and there a glorious smash,
And a hundred killed and wounded,—
It's little our jolly Directors care
For a passenger's neck if he pays his fare,
· Away you go at a florin the pair,
The signal whistle has sounded !'

    .   .   .   .   .

Off at last !
An hour past
The time, and carriages tight-full ;
Why this should be
We don't quite see,
But of course it's all a part of the spree
And it's really most delightful !

(CHORUS.)

Crash, crack,
Brighton and back,
All the way for a shilling,—

Tho' the speed be slow,
We're likely to go
A long journey before we get back d'you know,
The pace is so wonderfully ' killing' !

Ho ! 'slow' d'you find?
Then off, like the wind—
With a jerk that to any unprejudiced mind
Feels strongly as if it had come from *behind*—
Away like mad we clatter ;
Bang—slap,—bang—rap,—
' Can't somebody manage to see what has hap—— ?'
There goes Jones's head !—no, it's only his cap --
Jones, my boy, who's your hatter?

Slow it is, is it? jump jolt,
Slithering wheel and starting bolt,
Racketing, reeling, and rocking,—
Now we're going it !--jolt jump,
Whack thwack, thump bump,—
It's a mercy we're all stuck fast in a lump,
The permanent way is shocking !

(CHORUS.)

Jump, jolt,
Engines that bolt,
Brighton and back for a shilling

Jolt jump-- but we're children and wives,
Thump bump— who value our lives,
And you won't catch one here again who survives
The patent process of killing;

(CHORUS OF DIRECTORS.)

With our slap dash, crack crash,
And here and there a glorious smash,
   And a hundred killed and wounded!—
It's little we jolly Directors care
For a passenger's limbs if he pays his fare,
So away you go at a florin the fair,
   The signal whistle has sounded!

WANTED—AN IDEA.

YOU want an idea? then I've got it !—
 Prepared to impart on the spot :
  You'll probably think
  The idea's for a Rink
Or a Bank or Bazaar ?—but it's not.

Not at all ! I disclaim all designs
Philanthropic, past, future, or present :
  So of course you'll suppose
  It's a Poem or Prose,
Or a Sermon or Song ? -but it isn't.

Then you'd guess it was something in Art
Or in Science—that should be, or shouldn't —
  'Twould be something that's new,
  Or at least something true—
Something somehow, you know ?—but it wouldn't !

No, no ! F.R.S. and R.A.,
This idea isn't what you call ' *savant* '—
  Not Tyndall or ' Phiz '—
  My idea of it is
That I've got an idea that *—you haven't.*

QUACK! QUACK!! QUACK!!!

First Patient.

OH, doctor dear, make haste !
Give me something nice to taste -
I'm bent like a ball
With what you may call
A headache in the waist.

First Quack.

I'll give you a box of PILLS —
They cure all earthly ills
Take ten at a time
You'll find it sublime
(If it doesn't cure it kills.)

Second Patient.

Oh, doctor, I shall die !
I've just poked out my eye—
It's black as a nigger
And five times bigger
Than the biggest gooseberry pie !

Second Quack.

I give you a splendid LOTION
(What it does I haven't a notion),
   Keep mopping it fast,
   You'll find out at last
The plan of perpetual motion.

Third Patient.

Help, doctor dear, I beg !
I want screwing up a ' peg '—
   From the top of St. Paul
   I happened to fall
And fractured my dexter leg !

Third Quack.

I'll give you an OINTMENT of power
You'll rub it in for an hour—
   (If you fancy it, *two*—
   It's amusing for you
And won't hurt—it's tallow and flour).

Chorus of Quacks and Patients.

This world's all take and give,
One dies that t'other may live,
   And fools for knaves
   Drop into their graves
As sand drops through a sieve !

AN UNINVITED GUEST.

THE supper and the song had died
 When to my couch I crept ;
I flung the muslin curtains wide
And took a ' first-class place inside '
 It might have seemed I slept.

Yet scarce the drowsy god had woo'd
 My pillow to befriend,
When fancy, how extremely rude ?
A fellow evidently screw'd
 Got in, *the other end !*

The bolster from my side he took
 To make his own complete,
Then sat, and gazed with scornful look, —
With wrath my very pulses shook
 And quivered to my feet.

I kicked of course — long time in doubt
 The war waged to and fro ;
At last I kicked the rascal out
And woke — to find explosive gout
 Developed in my toe.

AH, WHO?

WHO comes so damp by grass and grave
    At ghastly twilight hour,
And bubbles forth his pois'nous breath
    On ev'ry shudd'ring flow'r?

Who dogs the houseless wanderer
    Upon the wintry wold;
And kisses—with his frothy lips—
    The clammy brow and cold?

Who, hideous, trails a slimy form,
    Betwixt the moonlight pale,
And the pale, fearful, sleeping face?——
    Our little friend—the Snail.

'THE WORLD'S MINE OYSTER.'

'THE world's mine oyster !' but, alas !
   No other oyster's in my reach ;
Oh, friends, how does it come to pass
   That you've arrived at threepence each ?

Time was—away, bewildering thought !
   The fancy sets my pulses thrilling—
A dozen 'natives' might be bought,
   With bread and butter, for a shilling . .

But these are glories of the past,
   We hardly wonder where they've got to ;
A generation's coming fast
   Won't even 'recollect the grotto,'—

And when that old New Zealand swell
   Arrives on London bridge to pose,
He'll find the final oyster-shell
   Suspended from Britannia's nose.

H ERR BELLOWS, won't you sing?
   (Or rather won't you *roar?*—)
I should like so to accompany you—
   (As far as the street door) . . .

Miss Squeals will take her part
   In that charming duet by Meyer,
With Signor Buffo? (that's *two* at a go,
   I wish I could do them in ' choir ! ')

Lord Whooper sings, I know?
   (Too well! and always flat)—
What an exquisite air—(for a dirge on the stair
   Assisted by the cat !) . . .

Shan't we hear *your* voice, madame?
   (Be thanked ! she's a cold in the head—)
Pray pity our loss —(what a fool I was !
   She's going to ' play instead ') . . .

' Encore?' (oh, I can't stand this—
   They're going it, ' hammer and tongs '
Confound them all ! I'll get out in the hall
   And leather away at the gongs !)

ON GHOSTS.

I'M not much set on ghosts altho' no doubt
  Psychologists may feel a predilection
For such ' leave-ticket' gentry, loose about
  In history and fiction ;—

Familiar spirits, loved but *never* lost !
  Like that vex'd shade in Corsica's twin Brothers,
Or in Macbeth, Don Juan, Hamlet, Faust,
  And half a hundred others :

Of which, N.B., not half are ghosts at all,
  But nondescripts defying diagnosis,
Tho' Mrs. Crowe herself the list should call
  Of each metempsychosis.

Faust's Mephistopheles, who filch'd his soul,
  Was just a ' psychic' with a kleptomania,
(In this resembling Oberon—who stole
  The changeling of Titania—)

Ondine's a ' Nymph,' who wanted to be kissed
  And didn't, both at once—case not uncommon,
And, barring ' tragics,' it must be confessed
  A rather nice young woman :

Ariel's a puzzle, or has always been
 To me—altho' the part plays neatly, very,—
But then it's only fair to add I've seen
 It acted by Kate Terry :

[' Delicate Ariel ! ' had I Prosp'ro's skill
 I would have work'd some charm to break my vow—
Yet keep it—and your sweet self singing still
 ' Under the hanging blossom on the bough ' !]

Avenel's White Lady of the Fountain, vex'd
 To see her girdle less'ning in dimension !
Proving herself at least a ghost unsex'd—
 No sprite of Eve's invention :

Witches ar'n't ghosts, or ghosts still in the flesh,
 Altho' they ride on broomsticks over ditches ;
And this being thus, the point that's raised afresh
 Is to tell which is witches?

A Sylphide's what—I know not—not *a-miss*—
 Nor fragile Peri from a rose-leaf sipping,
Mermaids and Naiads wear a charming dress
 But run too much to ' dripping.'

Then there's the Dry-ad, just by way of change,
 Brownie and Banshee, Troll   but he's a woodfellow -
Fays, Elves, and Sprites who toadstool rings arrange
 And Puck or Robin Goodfellow ;—

Kelpie and Kobold, Wraith, and Spook, and Pix,
  Hobgoblin, Imp, and things of smaller matter
Not worth invoking—Bogie, Gnome, and Nix,
  ' Hyperion to a Satyr.' . . .

And still they come ! they come before I call—
  Indeed, I'd no idea so vast their bulk was.
' I'll see no more ! ' give me, if ghosts at all,
  Ghosts solid, as ' Fitzfulk ' was.

POSTSCRIPT TO GHOSTS.

I T seems that after all some friends have got
    Left in the lurch, to favour rhyme or brevity—
The apparitions mean to make it hot
    For treating them with levity.

A Siren hints I must have lost my eyes,
    A Harpy kindly lets me know I'm ' wanted,'
A Houri threatens me with Paradise,
    A Hag with being haunted.

If this were all I might p'raps ' chance the ducks,'
    But there's a Vampyre making frightful faces ;
A Ghoul has routed all my guardian Pucks
    And offers its embraces. . . .

So there,—now, let's make peace ! But, when all's done,
    These kind won't ' act ' with Edmund Phelps or
        Fechter,
At least your genuine Ghost had got some fun,
    The real Shakspearian Spectre.

The King of Denmark was a gallant soul
   Fresh run from Styx, and lively as a samlet,
'Twas Hamlet's uncle murder'd the ' old mole,
   And Fechter murder'd Hamlet -)

And honest too, or honester than most,
   Who what he owed his brother came and paid him
As for Macbeth but stay, he's not a ghost,
   Or Irving would have laid him ! . . .

And so adieu, sweet friends going, going, *gone !*
   I have enshrined you in a splendid ditty,
And won't be haunted more by any one. . . .
   Unless they're young and pretty.

DERBY DAY.

OH ! who will over the Downs with me?
    Over Epsom Downs, and away—
The Sun has got a tear in his eye,
And the morning mists are light and high ;—
    We shall have a splendid day.

   .   .   .   .   .   .

And splendid it is, by all that's hot !—
    A regular blaze on the hill ;
And the turf rebounds from the light-shod heel
And the tapering spokes of the delicate wheel
With a springy-velvety sort of a feel
    That fairly invites 'a spill.'
    Splendid, I say, but we mustn't stop,
    The folks are beginning to run :
Is yonder a cloud that covers the course?
No, it's fifty thousand—man and horse—
    Come out to see the fun.

   .   .   .   .   .   .

So—just in time for the trial spin ;
    The jocks are cantering out,—
We shall have the leaders round in a crack,

And a hundred voices are shouting 'back,'
    But nobody stirs a foot !
   There isn't a soul will budge
  So much as an inch from his place,
Tho' the hue of the Master's scarlet coat
    Is a joke compared to his face. . . .
  'To the ropes ! to the ropes !'—
    Now stick to your hold,—
  A breezy flutter of crimson and gold,
    And the crowd are swept aside,—
You can see the caps as they fall and rise
Like a swarm of variegated flies
    Coming glittering up the ride ;
'To the ropes, for your life ! . . . Here they come .
  there they go –'
    The exquisite graceful things !
In the very sport of their strength and pride :
Ha ! that's the Favourite—look at his stride,
    It suggests the idea of wings :
  And the glossy neck is arched and firm
    In spite of the flying pace ;
The jockey sticks to his back like glue,
And his hand is quick and his eye is true,
And whatever skill and pluck can do
    They will do to get the race.
  The colt with the bright broad chest,
    Will run to win to-day ···

There's fame and fortune in every bound
And a hundred and fifty thousand pound
    Staked on the gallant Bay !

   .   .   .   .   .   .

      ' *They're off !* ' . . . .
   And away at the very first start,
   ' Hats down ! hats down in front !
' Down there, you sir in the wide-awake ! '
The tightened barriers quiver and shake,
   But they bravely bear the brunt.

A hush, like death, is over the crowd——
   D'you hear that distant cry ? . . .
Then hark how it gathers, far and near,
One rolling, ringing, rattling cheer
   As the race goes dashing by,
And away with the hats and caps in the air,
   And the horses seem to fly ! . . .

Forward ! forward ! at railway speed,
There's one that has fairly taken the lead
   In a style that can scarce miscarry ;
Over and on, like a flash of light,
And now his colours are coming in sight,
Favourite ! Favourite ! scarlet and white —
   He'll win, by the Lord Harry ! !

If he can but clear the Corner, I say,
 The Derby is lost and won—
It's a fearful shave, but he'll do the trick,
Now! Now! -well-ridden—he's passing it quick. —
He's round! . . .
 No, he isn't ; he's broken his neck,
  And the jockey his collar-bone :
And the whirlwind race is over his head,
Without stopping to ask if he's living or dead,
 Was there ever such rudeness known ?
He fell like a trump in the foremost place
He died with the rushing wind on his face -
At the wildest bound of his glorious pace--
 In the mad exulting revel ;
He left his shoes to his son and heir,
His hocks to a champagne dealer at Ware,
  A lock of his hair
  To the Lady-Mare,
And his hoofs and tail——to the devil.

TRIALS OF A DYSPEPTIC.

'LUNCH, sir? yes-ser, pickled salmon,
　　Cutlets, Kidneys, Greens, and '——Gammon !
Have you got no wholesome meat, sir?
Flesh or fowl that one can eat, sir?
' Eat, sir? yes-ser, on the dresser
Pork, sir '—Pork, sir, I detest, sir—
' Lobsters?'　Are to me unblest, sir—
' Duck and Peas?'　I can't digest, sir—
' Puff, sir?'　Stuff, sir!　' Fish, sir?'　Pish, sir!
' Sausage?'　Sooner eat the dish, sir—
' Shrimps, sir? prawns, sir? crawfish? winkle?
' Scallops ready in a twinkle?
　　　' Wilks and cockles, crabs to follow !'
　　　Heav'ns, *nothing* I can swallow ! . . .

WAITAR !

' *YES - SAR.*'

Bread for twenty —
I shall starve in midst of plenty !

ON THE RINK.

Ce n'est que le premier pas qui coûte.

YES, it's awfully nice, and all that sort of thing,
  But please take me back to a seat,—
Your intentions are excellent, Guy, I am sure,
But oh ! may you never be forced to endure
  The anguish I feel in my feet !

These straps are too tight - or the wheels don't go right
  And my ankles are cut like a knife,—
Young Larkins pursues me wherever I go,
And ' cannons '— it must be on purpose, I know,
  For he never collides with his wife !

Bumped battered and bruised, kicked cuffed and ill-used,
  I'm a ' figure for fun ' (or for ' Punch ')—
So now that you've taken my skates off, dear Guy,
And I feel less immediately likely to die,
  We'll adjourn *au revoir*, after lunch !

ECHOES FROM THE SAME.

First Echo.　*Agitato.*

YOU see me just now on my knees
　　And my elbows, and that's because
I arose in my strength—
To re-measure my length
　　On the spot where I previously was.

Second Echo.　*Flatanato.*

If I don't rise to take off my hat,
　　I beg you won't think me a clown,—
On occasions like these
One ' stands at one's ease '
　　Most easily lying down.

Third Echo.　*Soffogato.*

It's pleasant to tumble at times—
　　(The times when one's ready to drop),
He felt this as well,
The elderly swell
　　Who's floored me and sits on the top. . .

FOURTH ECHO. *Curvalato.*

I am stooping my balance to gain ;
  Anon I shall backward descend ;
And that's what I call
My Roman fall
  And alternate Grecian bend.

SUNDRY ECHOES. *Dislocato.*

What Splice-bone says is true —
  The ' exercise ' is good —
But he might have added
Get your legs padded,
  And elbows made of wood.

REJECTED ADDRESSES.

S IR Toby was a portly party ;
  Sir Toby took his turtle hearty ;
  Sir Toby lived to dine :
Château margot was his fort ;
Bacchus would have backt his port ;
He was an Alderman in short
  Of the very first water—and wine.

An Alderman of the first degree,
But neither wife nor son had he :
  He had a daughter fair, —
And often said her father, ' Cis,
' You shall be dubbed "my Lady," Miss,
  ' When I am dubbed Lord Mayor.

' The day I don the gown and chain,
' In Hymen's modern Fetter-lane,
  ' You wed Sir Gobble Grist ;
' And whilst I strut, and star it by
' St. George's in the East, you'll try
  ' St. George's in the West.'

Oh, vision of paternal pride !
Twice blessed Groom to such a Bride !

Thrice happy Lady Cis !
Yet sparks won't always strike the match,
And miss may chance to lose her ' catch,'
    Or he may catch - a *miss !*

Such things do happen, here and there,
When knights are old, and nymphs are fair,
    And who can say they don't ?
When Gouty takes the gilded pill,
And Dives stands and says ' *I will*,'
    And Beauty says ' *I won't* ! '

Sweet Beauty ! Sweeter thus by far
Young Goddess of the silver star,
    Divinity capricious !—
Who would not barter wealth and wig,
And pomp and pride and *otium dig*,
For Youth—when ' plums ' weren't worth a fig,
    And Venus smiled propitious ?

Alas ! that beaus will lose their spring,
And wayward belles refuse to ' ring,'
    Unstruck by Cupid's dart !
Alas that must the truth be told—
Yet oft'ner has the archer sold
The ' white and red,' to touch the ' gold,'
    And Diamonds trumped the Heart !

That luckless heart ! too soon misplaced !
Why is it that parental taste
On sagest calculation based
 So rarely pleases Miss ?
Let those who can the riddle read ;
For me, I've no idea indeed,
 No more, perhaps, had Cis.

It might have been she found Sir G.
Less tender than a swain should be,—
 Young —sprightly - witty—gay ?—
It might have been she thought his hat
Or head too round or square or flat
 Or empty—who can say ?

I know not ! But the Parson waited,
The Bridegroom swore, the Groomsmen rated,
 Till two o'clock or near ;—
Then home again in rage and wrath,
Whilst pretty Cis was rattling North
 With Jones the Volunteer.

ANTI-ANTIQUARIAN.

D O I dote upon ' desolate towers ? '
    I really can't say that I do ;
They afford no protection from showers,
    But copious cobwebs and dew.

These courts (do you ever play tennis ?)
    Are Norman ?—No, Saxon, I'm sure :
That arch Saracenic ? at Venice
    And Cairo I've seen some before.

Let them sleep with their founders below them
    Your antediluvian stones
Won't stop an east wind howling thro' them
    That's chilling one into the bones.

My taste doesn't run upon gables
    Nor buttresses old as the flood :
I'd rather put faith in ' Last Fables '
    Than the dates of Professor Macmud.

' Stone Facts ' I believe to be fiction
    ' Rock Records ' afford me no joy,
No, I haven't the least predilection
    For desolate towers, old boy.

HAUNTED.

DID you never hear a rustling
 In the corner of your room ;
When the faint fantastic fire-light
 Served but to reveal the gloom ?
Did you never feel the clammy
 Terror, starting from each pore,
  At a shocking
  Sort of knocking
On your chamber door ?

Did you never fancy something
 Horrid, underneath the bed ?
Or a ghastly skeletonian,
 In the garret overhead ?
Or a sudden life-like movement,
 Of the ' Vandyke,' grim and tall ?
  Or that ruddy
  Mark, a bloody
Stain upon the wall ?

Did you never see a fearful
 Figure, by the rushlight low ?

Crouching, creeping, crawling nearer
  Putting out its fingers—*so!*
Whilst its lurid eyes glared on you
  From the darkness where it sat—
      And you could not,
      Or you would not,
    See it was the cat?

THE BLOATED BIGGABOON.

THE bloated Biggaboon,
    Was so haughty, he would not repose
In a house, or a hall, or *ces choses*,
But he slept his high sleep in his clothes—
    'Neath the moon.

The bloated Biggaboon
Pour'd contempt upon waistcoat and skirt,
Holding swallow-tails even as dirt—
So he puff'd himself out in his shirt,
    Like a b'loon.

IN MEDIÆVOS.

IF you love to wear
 An unlimited extent of hair
Push'd frantically back behind a pair
Of ears, that all asinine comparison defy·
 And peripatate by star light
 To gaze upon some far light
Till you've caught an aggravated catarrh right
In the pupil of your frenzy rolling eye,--
 Or if you're given to the style
 Of that mad fellow Tom Carlyle,
And fancy all the while, you're taking 'an earnest view'
 of things,--
 Making Rousseau a hero,
 Mahomet any better than Nero,
And Cromwell an angel in ev'rything except the wings :
 Or if you weep sonnets,
 Over TIME, and on its
Everlasting works of 'art' and 'genius' (cobweb
 wreathed !)
 And fly off into rapture
 At some villanous old picture
 Not an atom like nature
Nor any human creature, that ever breathed,

Some Amazonian Vixen
Of indescribable complexion
And hideous all conception to surpass ;
And actually prefer this abhorrence
To a lovely portrait by Sir Thomas Lawrence-
Why then, dear reader--you must be an Ass !

NAUGHTY TWO-SHOES.

AT SKIPPINGTON.

PRETTY naughty Two-shoes
    Bought a pair of blue shoes,
Bought a pair of silken hose all striped with white and
    red ;
    Bought a skipping rope for skipping—
    When they threatened her with whipping
Skipt them straightway into kissing her instead.

    Skipt them into such ecstatics
    That they thronged from base to attics
Peeping out from garret-window, pane, and door ;
    Skipt the bumpkins out of wits,
    Skipt their sweethearts into fits,
Skipt them higher than was ever seen before.

    Basta ! cried the lame schoolmaster
    But she only skipt the faster ;
With her beautiful kaleidoscopic feet ;

From the squire to the clown
Skipt the village upside down,—
And I doubt if it has ever righted yet !

THE 'MATRIMONIAL NEWS.'

A YEAR ago with pockets full
   My steps would often range,
To do a modest ' bear ' or ' bull,'
From Grub Street to th' Exchange ;
Sometimes my glance was golden-hued--
   Sometimes I'd got the blues, —
      But smile or frown
      Could not put down
The ' Matrimonial News.'

' I say, sir ! Marry ? Want a wife ? '--
' The Devil '—' Here you are ! '
' Just only buy the 'News and try '——
   ' Avaunt ! '—' *A penny ! !* ' . . ' BAH ! ! ! '

And now, you know, I'm really wed,
   Perhaps I took the hint ?—
At all events I'm fairly rid
   Of that obnoxious print ;

For since the hour I gave the ring
   All note the brats refuse,
No youthful tout now spreads me out
   The ' Matrimonial News.'

It can't be in my cut of coats, —
I'm not increasing fat, —
I still wear Hoby-Humby's boots
And Lincoln-Bennet's hat,
And thro' a single eye-glass squint
The most benignant views ;—
But frown or smile
I can't beguile
The ' Matrimonial News ! '

TOO BAD, YOU KNOW.

I T was the huge metropolis
    With fog was like to choke ;
It was the gentle cabby-horse
    His ancient knees that broke ;—

And, oh, it was the cabby-man
    That swore with all his might,
And did request he might be blowed
    Particularly tight,
If any swell should make him stir
    Another step that night !

Then up and spake that bold cabman,
    Unto his inside Fare,
' I say, you Sir, come out of that ! –
    ' I say, you Sir, in there—

' Six precious aggrawatin miles
    ' I've druv to this here gate,
' And that poor injered hanimal
    ' Is in a fainting state ;

'There ain't a thimblefull of light,
　'The fog's as black as pitch,—
'I'm flummox'd 'tween them posteses
　'And that most *'ateful* ditch.

'So bundle out ! my 'oss is beat ;
　'I'm sick of this 'ere job ;—
'I say, you Sir in there,—d'you *hear?*

　　.　　.　　.　　.　　.

'*He's bolted--strike me bob !*'

NEXT MORNING.

IF some one's head's not very bright,
  At least the owner bears no malice. . .
Who was it pulled my nose last night,
  And begged an interview at Calais?

The quarrel was not much, I think,
  For such a deadly arbitration,
Some joke about the ' missing link '
  And all the rest inebriation.

In vino veritas! which means
  A man's a very ass in liquor ;
The ' thief that slowly steals our brains '
  Makes nothing but the temper quicker.

Next morning brings a train of woes,
  But finds the passions much sedater—
Who was it, now, that pulled my nose ?—
  I'd better ring and ask the waiter.

VENI, VIDI, VICI.

(FIRST LETTER FROM COTTONSHIRE.)

. . . . .

A N unfledged heiress in her 'teens,
　　And worth a Plum they say ;
With charms to move an anchorite—
The Count made running at first sight,
　　But didn't seem to ' stay : '
I mean to-night to wire in.
No ' roping ' dodges –run to win
　　You know my slashing way ;
　　The *veni, vidi, vici* style,
　　Short, sharp, decisive, ch ?

I'll send you up the ' stuff' to square
　　That Epsom score I owe—
Once get the Heiress well in hand,
Old Cent. per cent. is sure to stand
　　Another thou' or so ;
For when all's said and done, you see,
　　There's nothing like the R. M. D.
　　That makes the mare to go . . .

So now to cage this golden dove,
And lime these unfledg'd wings with love—
   Yoick, forward ! Tally-ho !

.   .   .   .   .

.   .   .   .   .   .

(SECOND LETTER.)

It's all U. P., old man,—'unfledged !'
   (Could laugh if 'tweren't for spite)—
Unfledged as falcon when he springs !
She'll teach them all to 'lime their wings'
   And try their claws, the kite !
She's up to every move that's out,
Knows when to sigh and smile and pout
And ' plays' you, as you'd play a trout—
   The more fool I to bite ! . . .

At first she seemed to like the ' pace '
   And answer'd to the bit,
Blushed when I praised her twinkling feet,
Whilst all her eyes grew dark and sweet—
   Green eyes with mischief lit,—
' I'm like a grape from the rich South,
(They said) to drop into your mouth—
   Why don't you open it ?' . . .

I clasped her jewelled hand in mine
   And through the gallop flew,

Her slender waist my arm compressed,
Her whispered words almost caressed,—
    ' Another turn or two ! '—
And the lights flashed and music crashed—
    (Here the scene changed, you know).

I led her drooping to a seat
    Beside the ferny fount,—
I murmured, Hearts are more than gold !
She smiled, ' So I've been often told,'
Then hear me swear by all I hold—
    ' No, please, I think I won't ! '
Ah, les yeux verts, les yeux d'enfer !—
(One effort more, my boy, to win)
You do not care for me a pin !
    She laugh'd —' Of course I don't ! '
Then gently yawning . . . ' Thanks—ta-ta ! '—
And left me speechless, *planté là.* . . .
      (P.S.)
The minx has hooked the Count.

THE RATTLE-SNAKES' CONGRESS.

'O WAKEN snakes!' a herald cried,
 'Attend to what I say;
The bearer of a proclamation
To all the elders of the nation,
 Oyez! oyez!! oyez!!!'

'To all long-suff'ring Rattle-snakes
 Whom indignation pales,
That we alone of serpent kind
An instrument of music find
 Appended to our tails.'

'Thrice hateful " bones!" attracting all
 That snakey paths molest;
That warn mankind to clear the course
And often waken up perforce
 Ourselves from peaceful rest.'

'You see for want of sleep by day
 We all look wan and white,—
Condemn'd by every thoughtful snake
The whole arrangement's a mistake
 And odious in our sight.'

' Wherefore . . . a Parliament is fixed
    In crotalus, straightway,
To legislate upon the point
How to curtail this caudal joint
    Oyez ! Oyez ! ! Oyez ! ! ! '

' The day was set, the Congress met '
    Prepared for wordy battle ;
Alas ! detractors have averr'd
That not a sound was ever heard —
    Save one stupendous rattle !

CHINESE PUZZLES.

THE WEDDING GIFT.

FROM many a dark delicious ripple
    The Moonbeams drank ethereal tipple,
Whilst over Eastern grove and dell
The perfumed breeze of evening fell,
And the young Bulbul warbling gave
Her music to the answ'ring wave.

But not alone the Bulbul's note
Bade Echo strike her silver lute,
Nor fell the music of her dream
Alone on waving wood and stream,
For thro' the twilight blossoms stray'd
Enamour'd youth, and faery maid,
And mingled with her warblings lone
A voice of sweet and playful tone.

'Nay, tell me not of love that lights
   'The diamond's midnight mine,—
'The cold sea-gleaming of the pearl
   'Is only half divine ;

M

' No thought have I for gold or gem,
    ' No 'hest of high emprize ;
' No giant Tartars to be slain,
    ' In homage to my eyes.'

Oh, take my life ! her lover cried –
    Nor break my dream of bliss ;
Take house, or head, or lands, or fame —
    Take ev'ry thing but *this*, —
To gaze upon your silken braids
    Unenvied be my part ;
I could not steal one golden tress,
    To bind it round my heart.

The lady laughed a careless laugh, –
    ' While downward flows the river,
' The lover who bids for Zadie's heart
' And hand must make up his mind to part
    ' With THE GIFT—or part for ever ! '

Excruciating girl ! why pierce
    A heart that beats for thee !
How can you want a Lock for which
    You still must want the Key ?

Just think, if I should wear a wig,
    How would you like me, Zadie ?

I'm sure you'll give it up, my pig,
　Do—there's a gentle ladye !

The Maiden laugh'd a silv'ry laugh, –
　' The white stars set and shiver ;
' The lover who bids for Zadie's heart
' And hand must make up his mind to part
　' With THE GIFT—or part for ever ! '

ETCETERA.

THE stars were out on the lake,
  The silk sail stirr'd the skiff,
And faint on the billow, and fresh on the breeze,
The summer came up thro' the cinnamon trees
  With an odoriferous sniff;
There was song in the scented air,
And a light in the list'ning leaves,
The light of the myriad myrtle fly,—
When young Fo-Fum and little Fe-Fi
Came forth to gaze upon the sky—&c!

Oh! little Fe-Fi was fair,
With the wreath in her raven hair!
With white of lily and crimson of rose,
From her almond eyes, and celestial nose,
To the tips of her imperceptible toes, &c.

Fo-Fum stood tall, I wis,
  (May his shadow never be less!)
A highly irresistible male,
  The ladies turn'd pale
  At the length of his nail
And the twirl of his unapproachable tail, &c.

Now listen, Moon-mine, my Star!
 My Life! my little Fe-Fi,—
For over the blossom and under the bough
There's a soft little word that is whispering now
  Which I think you can guess if you try!
 In the bosom of faithful Fum,
 There's an anti-celebic hum,—
A little wee word Fe-Fi can spell,
Concluding with ' E,' and beginning with ' L ' &c.

  "Oh ! dear, now what can it be ?
  That little wee word Fo-Fum?
That funny wee word that sounds so absurd
  With an ' e ' and an ' l ' and a ' hum ' ?
 A something that ends with an E? . . .
 It must be my cousin, So-Sle ;
  Or pretty Zuzoo
 Who admired your queue ?——
I shall never guess what it can be
  I can see
That is spelt with an L and an E ? "

 Then listen, Moon-mine, my Life,
  My innocent little Fe-Fi ;
 It isn't So-Sle, tho' she ends with an E,
  And pretty Zuzoo
 Who approved of my queue,
  Has no L in her name that I see ;

In the bosom of faithful Fum,
It's a monosyllabic hum ;
A sweet little word for sweet lips to try,
That's half-and-half moonlight, and earth-light and sky,
If little Fe-Fi
Will open her mouth with the least little sigh
She must speak it—unless she was dumb !

" Indeed ! then perhaps she *is* dumb . . .
I vow I detest you Fo-Fum ! . . .
Why don't you . . . how *dare* you, I mean, sir . . . ah
me !
I shall never guess what it can be
I can see
That is spelt with an L and an E !
I never shall guess, if I die—
Fo-Fum, sir, I'm going to cry !—
Oh dear, how my heart is beginning to beat ! . . .
Why there's silly Fo-Fum on his knees at my feet," &c.

Deponent knoweth not,
History showeth not,
If the lady read the riddle ;
And whether she found
It hard to expound—
As the story ends in the middle.

Was gallant Fo-Fum
Constrained to succumb
To the thrall of delicious fetters?—
Or pretty Fe-Fi
Induced to supply
The text of the missing letters?

Oh, no one can tell!
But this extract looks well,
Faute de mieux (that's ' for want of a betterer'
' Received : by Hang-Hi,
' From Fo-Fum, for Fe-Fi,
' A thousand dollars,' &c !

WHAT THE PRINCE OF I DREAMT.

I DREAMT it ! such a funny thing —
    And now it's taken wing ;
I s'pose no man before or since
    Dreamt such a funny thing ?

It had a Dragon ; with a tail ;
    A tail both long and slim,
And ev'ry day he wagg'd at it——
    How good it was of him !

And so to him the tailest
    Of all three-tailed Bashaws,
Suggested that for reasons
    The waggling should pause :

And held his tail—which, parting,
    Reversed that Bashaw, which
Reversed that Dragon, who reversed
    Himself into a ditch.

.   .   .   .   .   .

It had a monkey in a trap—
    Suspended by the tail :
Oh ! but that monkey look'd distress'd,
    And his countenance was pale.

And he had danced and dangled there ;
  Till he grew very mad :
For his tail it was a handsome tail
  And the trap had pinched it—bad.

The trapper sat below, and grinn'd ;
  His victim's wrath wax'd hot :
He bit his tail in two   and fell—
  And kill'd him on the spot.

  .   .   .   .   .   .

It had a pig   a stately pig ;
  With curly tail and quaint :
And the Great Mogul had hold of that
  Till he was like to faint.

So twenty thousand Chinamen,
  With three tails each at least,
Came up to help the Great Mogul,
  And took him round the waist.

And so, the tail slipp'd through his hands ;
  And so it came to pass,
That twenty thousand Chinamen
  Sat down upon the grass.

  .   .   .   .   .   .

It had a Khan—a Tartar Khan—
  With tail superb, I wis ;
And that fell graceful down a back
  Which was considered his.

Wherefor all sorts of boys that were
    Accursèd, swung by it ;
Till he grew savage in his mind
    And vex'd, above a bit :

And so, he swept his tail, as one
    Awak'ning from a dream ;
And those abominable ones
    Flew off into the stream.

Likewise they bobbled up and down,
    Like many apples there ;
Till they subsided—and became
    Amongst the things that were.

    .   .   .   .   .   .

And so it had a moral too,
    That would be bad to lose ;
' Whoever takes a Tail in hand
    Should mind his p's and queues.' . . .

I dreamt it !—such a funny thing !
    And now it's taken wing ;
I s'pose no man before or since
    Dreamt such a funny thing?

FINIS.

Spottiswoode & Co., Printers, New-street Square, London.

PUCK ON PEGASUS.

TWELFTH THOUSAND. Price 2s. 6d.

Illustrated by Sir Noel Paton, Millais, Leech, Tenniel, Doyle, &c.

Press Criticisms on former Editions.

'Splendid verse. . . . The sixth edition—on the merits of the book it ought to be the sixtieth. . . . Those who do not already know the wonderful swing of Mr. Cholmondeley-Pennell's lines should make their acquaintance at once.'—STANDARD.

'Extravagant mirth expressing itself in easy running verses, the music of which is as sweet as these rhymes are ingenious and unexpected. . . . The rhythm and rugged swing of the "Night Mail North" will give our readers a taste of Mr. Pennell's higher qualities.'
MORNING POST.

'There is no doubt that Mr. Cholmondeley-Pennell's "Puck on Pegasus," which has reached a sixth edition, merits the honour and success of that unquestionable proof of popularity. The book has been reviewed over and over again.'— DAILY TELEGRAPH.

'The epigrammatic drollery of Mr. Cholmondeley-Pennell's "Puck on Pegasus" is well known.'—TIMES.

'A beautiful and amusing book. . . . Mr. Pennell always shows himself a master of the art of versification.'—SCOTSMAN.

'The saddling of Pegasus, with Puck for rider, was almost an event both in the world of literature and in that of pictorial illustration. The book was full of talent, full of life. It ran over with the most genial fun, the heartiest humour; and in felicitous combination with these you had what, indeed, true humour and good fun can never dispense with masculine thought, vigorous sentiment, genuine pathos. The verse was vivacious without being trivial, sportive and sparkling without being frivolous. In "Puck on Pegasus" there was literary work which, of its kind, has perhaps never been surpassed: brilliant sketching of not unimportant aspects of life, piquant but unenvenomed satire, rhymed sense that reminded you of Thackeray, strokes of tenderness that reminded you of Hood.'
SPECTATOR.

'Clever and amusing, vigorous and healthy. There is plenty of poetry in railways and steam engines, and now that other mines of inspiration are growing exhausted, we cannot see why a new shaft should not be run in this direction.'— SATURDAY REVIEW.

'"Puck on Pegasus" is full of those eccentricities which make one laugh *with* oneself, or *in spite* of oneself, according as one takes it up in a grave or gay humour.'—FRASER'S MAGAZINE.

'This is a sixth edition, but it might honestly be a sixteenth. . . Mr. Pennell often plays with his power, but there is the right stuff in almost every line he pens.'—THE FIELD.

'Let Mr. Pennell trust to the original strength that is in him, and he may bestride his Pegasus without fear.'--EXAMINER.

At all Libraries and Booksellers.

Now in preparation, a Revised Edition, price 4s. 6d.
MODERN BABYLON;
CRESCENT?, AND OTHER LYRICS.
Opinions of the Press.

'Language alike strong and musical. . . . Earnestness and fine appreciation of the grander qualities of nature, more especially of human nature, are on this occasion the chief characteristics of Mr. Pennell's muse. . . . "Crescent" is a passionate protest against the complaint ever on the lips of idlers, but scouted by all honest workers, that the Age of Poetry is past. . . . the nervous and deep-rolling lines of "Crescent" would of themselves be a sufficient answer.'—ATHENÆUM.

'Mr. Pennell is a stalwart champion of his age, and in reading his ringing lines we feel that most assuredly there is a charm for the poet in even the most material of modern life. . . . The following comes from a master-hand. . . .'—JOHN BULL.

'Real and undoubted poetic talent.'—SCOTSMAN.

'"Modern Babylon" contains some sixteen poems, well calculated to show the versatility of the author's muse. . . . Mr. Pennell grasps his subject with the vigour of a man of genius, and he invariably works on the right side of the question. He is wholesome, earnest, thoughtful--a worshipper not only of the beautiful but the good. . . . In such poems as "Holyhead to Dublin" there is rush and swing in the verse, which make it audible as the pace of a horse or the clank of a steam-vessel. . . . Side by side with this strength we find grace and elegance and airy fancies.

'It is very exceptional to find a gentleman like Mr. Cholmondeley-Pennell capable of charming us with such verse as this, and yet so practically gifted that *Baily's Magazine* can say of him, "He is not only well known as a *Senior Angler*, but as one of the straightest riders and best shots in England."'
MORNING POST.

'The opening poem, "Modern Babylon," is worthy of the philosophy of threescore years of earthly sojourn. "The Two Champions" gives an exquisite poetic setting to a beautiful idea. "Fire" is a clear and incisive bit of word-painting. . . . There is not, in fact, a single piece in this volume which does not evidence knowledge of the springs of human nature, deep culture and study, allied to invariable purity of thought and expression. . . .'
WESTMINSTER GAZETTE.

'One or two of the poems in "Puck on Pegasus"--"The Night Mail North" and "The Derby Day"—displayed unusual vigour and vivid descriptive power. . . . The reader seemed hurried along and amazed by the swiftness and brightness of the verses; and it was felt that so much dash and skilfulness in rhyme heralded a new poet, who would be likely to become the Laureate of the active wonders of the present age. It was thought, however, by many of Mr. Pennell's friends that he could not write serious poetry; and we suppose he has issued the present volume to undeceive them. . . . The passage we quote below could only emanate from a real poet. . . .'--PUBLIC OPINION.

At all Libraries and Booksellers.

PEGASUS RE-SADDLED.

Press Criticisms on First Edition.

'Mercurial with the spirit of frolic and fun, fertile of fancy, and gifted with the rare merit of perfect rhythm and rhyme, the muse of Mr. Cholmondeley-Pennell is always versatile and vivacious. We are inundated with poems of extreme lugubriousness of theme, and so-called comic ones, which are positively a discredit to our generation. But, fortunately for our sanity, we have among us several pleasant writers, the disciples and followers of that lively school of verse of which one of the best masters was Praed. . . . That the author of " Pegasus Re-Saddled " may fairly take rank with Locker and Austin Dobson, a few quotations will readily prove. " Faite à Peindre " is the opening poem, and Mr. Pennell being one of those fortunate writers from whose pleasant pages you may read at random, not by selection, we quote it entire :—

" Made to be painted – a Millais might give
    A fortune to study that exquisite face.
The face is a fortune, a Lawrence might live
    Anew in each line of that figure's still grace. . .

The pose is perfection, a model each limb,
    From the delicate foot to the classical head ;
But the almond blue eyes with their smiling look dim,
    And lips to be *loved* want a trifle more red.

Statuesque ? no, a Psyche, let's say, in repose—
    A Psyche whose Cupid beseeches in vain ;
We sigh as the nightingale sighs to the rose,
    That declines (it's averr'd) to give sighs back again.

If the wind shook the rose?—then a shower would fall
    Of sweet-scented petals to gather who list ;
If a sigh shook my Psyche?–she'd yawn, that is all,
    She's made to be painted, and not to be kist."

' This is poetry of the butterfly order, airy, buoyant, fragile as porcelain and fragrant as violets. It stirs no deep emotion, but is pleasant and wholesome as the smell of hay or the ripple of cool, clear waters. Pegasus is restrained by a light hand, and shows off his paces in a lamb-like temper. " The Secret of Safety" reveals the doctrine of the male-trifler and the coquette in its native deformity :

" You ask me to declare the spell
    By which I sleep unhaunted slumbers ;
' Still fancy free, the secret tell?'
    The secret is, fair Floribel,
    That ' safety lies in numbers.'

It is not that my heart is tough,
    I dare not make such false confession,
Or that it's formed of such soft stuff,
It is not durable enough
    To take a firm impression :

But Beauty's like the bloom that flies,
  And Love's a butterfly that hasteth ;
From lip to lip the trifler hies,
  And sweet by sweet the garden tries,
    But each one only tasteth.

If long I loiter'd here, I know
  I might not sleep unhaunted slumbers —
At least 'twere rash to try, fair Flo' —
  So now I'm going to the Row,
    Where ' safety lies in numbers.' "

This is not only " excellent fooling," but the spirit of flirtation is here
as wise as Minerva, and gives an excellent recipe to avoid heart-
ache. " Pretty Puss," whose face and figure Du Maurier renders
so admirably in form and expression, is evidently a vixen—a shrew
requiring the caprice of a Petruchio to tame her. " Pretty Puss's "
Lothario is in perplexity, and by no means complimentary—

" . . I wish I were back in the cab ;
  There's something remarkably *cat-like* in Mab.
If stroked the right way you get plenty of purr,
  But claws, I've a fancy, lie hid in the fur." . . .

" A Little Beauty " is a pretty picture of an imperious girl,
christened by the charming name of Maud, an enchantress, red-
lipped, soft-eyed, with cheeks like a peach—

" Round and ripe and fruity."

To quote the author in praise of the artist—

" The pose is perfection."

' " Anti-Antiquarian " will recall to the reader days of anticipated
delight in dilapidated castles green with ivy and mosses, and fragrant
with wall-flowers, the day's result being a sore throat, a sprained
ankle, and a toothache worthy of the anathema of Burns :—

" Do I dote upon 'desolate towers'?
  I really can't say that I do ; . . . .
They afford no protection from showers,
  But copious cob-webs and dew."

The concluding poem is as good as the first, so that we may truly
pronounce the book to be good from first to last.'--MORNING POST.

' Mr. Cholmondeley-Pennell has re-saddled his " Pegasus " none
too soon. One has heard of his doings at Hurlingham and Cairo
since he gave the world his last book of verse : and his pen has not
been idle with respect to those matters of sport on which he writes
with equal cleverness and authority. But his muse has for too long
a time been either silent, or tuneful only in places where her strains
cannot be heard. . . . He is also a minstrel whose popularity is
attested by the number of his editions. Mr. Frederick Locker's
" London Lyrics " has not had a larger sale than Mr. Pennell's " Puck
on Pegasus " ; and though the success of the last-named book of
vers de société may be in some degree due to the excellence and
variety of its illustrations, the literary merits of the book would

have rendered it famous even if they had been unattended with the attractions of artistic embellishment.

'As much may be said of the present volume, which, whilst it sustains Mr. Pennell's reputation for literary adroitness and subtlety, resembles its precursor in being a book of ornament as well as a book of humorous verse. We cannot remember the book that affords ten finer specimens of Mr. Du Maurier's skill. The draughtsman's "Little Bo-Peep" is, perhaps, the loveliest of all the lovely children his pencil has called into existence; and his "Maud," with her saucy little face, as she stands with her elbow resting on a mantelpiece, and her eyes scrutinising the reader's countenance, is as piquant and winsome a damsel as we have ever beheld. Admirably characteristic, also, is the beauty of the frontispiece, of whom the author says:

> "Statuesque? no, a Psyche, let's say, in repose
> A Psyche whose Cupid beseeches in vain —
> We sigh as the nightingale sighs to the rose,
> That declines (it's averred) to give sighs back again.
> If the wind shook the rose?—then a shower would fall
> Of sweet-scented petals to gather who list—
> If a sigh shook my Psyche?—she'd yawn, that is all,
> She's 'made to be painted,' and not to be kissed."

Exquisitely comical, also, are some of Mr. Pennell's "Ricking Reminiscences," which afford the following examples of his ability to commemorate embarrassing positions :—

> "FIRST ECHO.
> You see me just now on my knees
> And my elbows, and that's because
> I arose in my strength
> To remeasure my length
> On the spot where I previously was.
>
> SECOND ECHO.
> If I don't rise to take off my hat,
> I beg you won't think me a clown,
> On occasions like these
> One stands at one's ease
> Most easily, lying down.
>
> THIRD ECHO.
> It's pleasant to tumble at times—
> (The times when one's ready to drop).
> He felt this as well,
> The elderly swell
> Who's floored me and sits on the top.
>
> FOURTH ECHO.
> I am stooping, my balance to gain :
> Anon I shall backward descend :
> And that's what I call
> My Roman fall
> And alternate Grecian bend.

SUNDRY ECHOES.

What Splice-bone says is true—
The ' exercise ' is good :
But he might have added,
Get your legs padded,
And elbows made of wood."

If we have said enough to intimate that the work abounds with good things, and with reasons why it should be found on drawing-room tables, we have done all that the exigencies of space permit us to do for Mr. Pennell's new book of frolic and fine drawing.'—GLOBE.

'In the light and genial pages of "Pegasus Re-Saddled," by Mr. H. Cholmondeley-Pennell, we find ourselves in the presence of a new and charming " Little Bo-Peep "—lost at a midnight ball but found again, and sketched by Du Maurier's graceful pencil ; or the reader can turn to " A Curl in a Letter," " Hunting a Slipper," take a turn with " Ghosts by a Materialist," or go through " Lady Bell's Catechism," or join in any other of the fifty little dainty excursions so pleasantly offered. Something of the admirable swing of verse, graceful drollery, and vigorous and healthy fun that marked " Puck " in his first flight on " Pegasus," are also to be found here.'
STANDARD.

' Vers de société are becoming very much the fashion. We have now a fresh collection of light and lively poems from the pen of Mr. H. Cholmondeley-Pennell, whose " Puck on Pegasus," published some years ago, gave evidence of considerable facility in this class of composition. The title of his new volume is "Pegasus Re-Saddled," with ten illustrations by Mr. Du Maurier. Something of sameness attaches to all verses of this character, and in reading Mr. Pennell's we are occasionally under a momentary impression that we are in company with the muse of Mr. Frederick Locker. Mr. Pennell, however, has his own reputation to sustain, and the latest flight of his Pegasus will probably sustain it.'—DAILY NEWS.

'A charming volume of vers de société, well worthy of its predecessor, and very beautifully illustrated by Mr. John Maurier, who is particularly successful in his half-shy, half-coquettish treatment of " Little Bo-Peep," described in the following lines :

" Little Bo-Peep has lost her sheep,
And some one or other's lost little Bo-Beep !
Or she'd never be wandering at twelve o'clock,
With a golden crook and a velvet frock,
    In a diamond necklace, in such a rout,
In diamond buckles, and high-heel'd shoes
(And a dainty wee foot in them too, if you choose,
    And an ankle a sculptor might rave about. . . .),
But I think she's a little witch, you know,
With her broomstick-crook and her high-heel'd shoe :
And the mischievous fun that flashes through
The wreaths of her amber hair– don't you?

No wonder the flock follows Bo-Peep,
Such a shepherd would turn all the world into sheep,
To trot at her heels and look up in the face
Of their pastor for goodness knows what—say for grace.
Her face that recalls in its reds and its blues
And its setting of gold 'Esmeralda' by Greuse.

There's Little Bo-Peep, dress, diamonds, and all,
As I met her last night at a fancy ball."

Nor has Mr. Cholmondeley-Pennell's peculiar humour deserted him,
as we could quote several poems to prove—"Faite à Peindre," "A
Case of Spoons," &c., &c., and a little poem we must give entire.
. . . .[" An Uninvited Guest "].

We can only refer our readers to the touching little poem sent to the
late Mr. Charles Buxton, M.P., with the horse "White-Mist," on
the author giving up hunting owing to an accident in the hunting-
field.' LIVERPOOL ALBION.

'The author of " Puck on Pegasus " (now in its seventh edition)
has again made his appearance with a companion volume, which is
in all respects worthy of its popular predecessor. Light, graceful,
and sparkling in character, while abounding in playful humour, it
contains, besides, an amount of melody, and an occasional depth of
tender feeling which shows the author's capabilities of achieving
still higher triumphs in the field of poesy. The bulk of the volume
. . . . contains the *crème de la crème* of fashionable numbers,
merrily strung together, while there are occasional pieces which will
hold their own with the finest lyrics of the day. Here is a little
gem, and one taken at random :

' A DAISY CHAIN.

The white rose decks the breast of May,
    The red rose smiles in June,
Yet autumn chills and winter kills,
    And leaves their stems alone ;
Ah, swiftly dies the garden's pride,
    Whose sleep no waking knows—
But my love she is the daisy
    That all the long year grows.

The early woods are gay with green,
    The fields are prankt with gold,
But fair must fade and green be greyed
    Before the year is old ;
The bluebell hangs her shining head,
    No more the oxlip blows—
But my love she is the daisy
    That all the long year grows.

N

Still deck, wild woods, your mantle green,
  All meads bright jewels wear,
Let show'rs of spring fresh violets bring
  And sweetness load the air :
Whilst summer boasts her roses red,
  And March her scented snows,
My love be still the daisy,
  And my heart whereon she grows."

Good as is the foregoing, take the following, which, for tender playful humour, can hardly be surpassed :—

"A LITTLE BEAUTY.

Maud's a naughty little girl,
Maudie's locks decline to curl,
    Spite all sense of duty ;
But they're *frisé'd* up instead
Round her saucy little head —
Round her cheeks of white and red —
    Maud's a little beauty !

Maud has got a roguish eye,
Maud has got a tender sigh,
    Laughters soft and flutey—
'Cherries ripe' her lips, I swear,
Did you ever know a pair
Say so plainly ' If you dare !'
    Maud, the little beauty !

Yet her lip you cannot reach,
Nor her cheek that's like a peach,
    Round and ripe and fruity ;
You can only look and sigh,—
I can only love, and try
To discern the reason why
    Maud's *my* little beauty."

The book abounds in such excellent *morceaux* ; and we may confidently predict for it as extensive a popularity as its predecessor.'
                              EDINBURGH COURANT.

At all Libraries and Booksellers.

www.ingramcontent.com/pod-product-compliance
Lightning Source LLC
Chambersburg PA
CBHW030608040726
47497CB00008B/2897